The
ROMANCING *of*
EVANGELINE
IPSWICH

Center Point
Large Print

Also by Marcia Lynn McClure and available from Center Point Large Print:

The Windswept Flame
The Visions of Ransom Lake
The Heavenly Surrender
The Light of the Lovers' Moon
Beneath the Honeysuckle Vine
The Whispered Kiss
The Stone-Cold Heart of Valentine Briscoe
The Highwayman of Tanglewood
A Cowboy for Christmas
A Bargained-For Bride
A Crimson Frost
The Prairie Prince
The Bewitching of Amoretta Ipswich
The Secret Bliss of Calliope Ipswich

**This Large Print Book carries the
Seal of Approval of N.A.V.H.**

The
Romancing
of
Evangeline
Ipswich

Marcia Lynn
McClure

Center Point Large Print
Thorndike, Maine

This Center Point Large Print edition
is published in the year 2021 by arrangement with
Distractions Ink.

The text of this Large Print edition is unabridged.
In other aspects, this book may vary
from the original edition.
Printed in the United States of America
on permanent paper.
Set in 16-point Times New Roman type.

ISBN: 978-1-63808-149-4

The Library of Congress has cataloged this record under
Library of Congress Control Number: 2021944093

To my beautiful, inspirational mother—
You fill my heart with love
and tender memories,
My mind with images of simpler,
more romantic times,
And my soul with faith, hope, and strength!
I love you so much, Mom!
~Marcia

• • •

The following is a short but lovely memory reminisced upon and quickly written down by my mother, Patsy Christine States Reed, in 1991. Her sweet, handwritten memories will forever continue to inspire me!

Winter was beautiful with snow, ice, and frost. Clear, crisp nights when, as the sun set, the sky would go through every shade of blue from pale blue to blue green to sky blue to royal blue to dark blue to black blue with the last rays of the sun at the sky blue and royal blue stages turning the clouds from white to gold to light pink to darker pink to gray. The stars would appear one by one—silvery, crisp, and distinct. The Milky

Way could be seen stretching across the heavens, and then a crescent or full moon would appear to light up the frost forming in the air and settling on the ground or the frost diamonds resting on the snow of a few days before.

Darkness would have set in before I got off the bus at night. I sometimes would walk from the bus stop to home on the snowplowed road with the moonlight glistening on the snow on both sides. Before I reached the driveway, I would smell fresh baked bread, the cinnamon of fresh baked sweet rolls, and pinto beans cooking. Ahh! There's not a person on earth who ever ate so well on a cold wintry night. For my after-school snack, Mom would let me have a small bowl of beans with lots of black pepper and a glass of good, cold, uncooked (unpasteurized) whole milk. Christmas is in the air. New Year's Day comes and goes. Soon spring is in the air again.

• • •

To the man of my dreams . . .
My husband, Kevin!

• • •

Psst: FYI, the name *LaMontagne* is pronounced *la-mawn-TAIN.*

CHAPTER ONE

"Another letter to your friend?" Mrs. Perry asked.

Evangeline nodded, smiling as she handed the letter to Mrs. Perry to post. "Yes. I try to respond as quickly as I'm able."

"You're a sweetheart, Evangeline Ipswich. No doubt about it," Mrs. Perry commented. "And how is your friend doin'? Bein' that she's expectin' her baby soon and all."

Evangeline frowned, wondering whether she should even share her knowledge of her friend Jennie's condition with Mrs. Perry. After all, though Mrs. Perry and her husband owned the general store in Meadowlark Lake and were quite good friends to Evangeline and her family, Sophia Perry didn't know Jennie personally. She paused then in answering, uncertain of the propriety of discussing Jennie's situation with a stranger to her.

However, Evangeline's concern for Jennie, coupled with her need for reassurance, made the determination for her, and she answered, "Not as well as we would all like to hear."

Mrs. Perry frowned, prodding, "Oh?"

Evangeline shook her head, sending a stray strand of raven hair that had escaped a hairpin cascading down over one shoulder. "No. In fact, the doctor has urged her to bed rest for the remainder of her time."

"Oh dear!" Mrs. Perry exclaimed in a whisper. It was obvious the woman's concern was sincere, and Evangeline was glad she'd chosen to confide in her regarding Jennie's state.

"Yes. It's very worrisome," Evangeline continued. "In fact, Jennie has asked me to . . ." She paused, for she couldn't reveal Jennie's request to Mrs. Perry—not when she hadn't even informed her own family about it.

"She asked you to what, dear?" Mrs. Perry asked, patiently waiting for Evangeline's response.

"To . . . to write to her as often as I can," Evangeline answered.

Mrs. Perry smiled and nodded. "I can well imagine what a great comfort your letters are to her. Why, I was laid up in bed for near to six weeks when I was expectin' my Culver. And he was a big baby when he finally came too—near to nine pounds, Culver was. And I know letters from my sister . . . well, they surely did give me somethin' to look forward to."

"I do hope so," Evangeline sighed. "I mean to say, I'm not even sequestered to bed rest, and I so look forward to each and every one of Jennie's letters."

"With all you've got goin' on to keep you busy, Evangeline Ipswich?" Mrs. Perry laughed.

"Why, that baby sister of yours probably keeps you runnin' hither and yon all day, especially now that both your other sisters are married." Mrs. Perry sighed. "Oh, I've never in all my life seen weddin's as romantic and beautiful as your father's and your two sisters' were. Why, it's been almost a year since Amoretta married that handsome Brake McClendon, hasn't it?" Without waiting for an answer, she prattled, "And your father, the honorable Judge Ipswich, married the beautiful gypsy from the woods, Kizzy. Not to mention Rowdy Gates takin' Calliope to wife just over three months past. And every one of those weddin's was just a dream!"

"Yes," Evangeline agreed, although somewhat disheartenedly. It was true, both of Evangeline's younger blood sisters, Amoretta and Calliope, were married, happily settled in with handsome, loving husbands. Even her own father, Lawson Ipswich, had remarried almost a year before— and to a young and beautiful woman who brought with her an adorable daughter, Shay.

Still, though her joy was overflowing for her sisters and her father, she inwardly worried that she would become the Spinster Ipswich, that no man would ever pursue her—at least, no man that she desired to pursue her.

"I hear Mr. Longfellow has been quite attentive to you, honey," the well-meaning proprietress of the general store ventured. "He's a very handsome man, Evangeline. And those two little girls of his are just as sweet as peaches!"

Evangeline blushed a little and felt her emerald-green eyes begin to fill with the excess moisture borne of disappointment. Floyd Longfellow had indeed made no attempt to hide the fact that he was wildly interested in Evangeline. But kind as Floyd was, he was Evangeline's own father's age. And though perhaps that should not have mattered to her, it did. Evangeline had felt the weight of responsibility far too long—often felt older than her mere twenty-two years should have her feel. And she wanted a younger man—a man who did not own the heavy burden of memories of two wives who had passed on to heaven far before their time.

Her own stepmother, Kizzy—the beautiful gypsy woman who had healed her father's heart and married him—was certainly much younger than Evangeline's father. But there was a difference in her own father and Floyd Longfellow. Lawson Ipswich still had a young heart and was strong, handsome, and virile. He flirted and teased his young wife, and Evangeline knew that when Kizzy and her father's new baby arrived in November, her father would be as energetic and as loving to him or her as he ever had been from Evangeline's birth down to having adopted little six-year-old Shay.

She could not think the same of Floyd

Longfellow—a lonely, haunted sort of man. Evangeline needed youthfulness. She'd had to grow up too fast and own too much responsibility when her own mother had passed away when she was a girl of only twelve. And Floyd Longfellow had two little girls of his own that needed nurturing and love. Though she wanted children, she wanted children of her own—babies born of love and with a vibrant father.

Therefore, though she felt guilt-ridden for not appreciating the fact that Floyd Longfellow would propose and marry her that very moment if she would only agree to it, she smiled at Mrs. Perry and said, "He's a very kind man, but . . . but . . ."

Mrs. Perry smiled with understanding, reached out, and clasped Evangeline's hand in her own. "Floyd *is* a very kind man," she affirmed. "And I'm sure that one day he'll find himself a very kind woman to help him through life." She patted Evangeline's hand and added, "So you let him find that woman one day, and go where your heart leads you, darlin'."

Evangeline sighed with relief. She smiled, thinking how kind Mrs. Perry was—what a dear friend she had become. Sophia Perry was always so kind to everyone, and the merry little lady with the sweet, round face was kindest of all to Evangeline. At least it seemed so to Evangeline. She always felt more cheerful after a visit with

11

Mrs. Perry. She had hair that looked as if it had been spun from cinnamon and sugar and the brightest smile in all of Meadowlark Lake. It was no wonder she made a body feel more hopeful and happy.

"Thank you, Mrs. Perry," Evangeline said in quiet gratitude. "I-I struggle so with a feeling of obligation toward the man."

Mrs. Perry sighed. "It's that sackcloth-and-ashes demeanor of his, I'm afraid. Makes a body feel simply miserable and gray and guilty, doesn't it?"

Evangeline giggled. She couldn't help herself in giggling, because Mrs. Perry had expressed Evangeline's feelings exactly. "It does," she admitted.

"And a beautiful young woman like you, Evangeline . . . you need strength and joy, hope, and a bit more muscle on a man than Floyd Longfellow can provide, I'm afraid," Mrs. Perry offered with a mischievous grin. "It's clear your sisters, Amoretta and Calliope, were both drawn to handsome, muscular men who passionately love them and bathe them in happiness. And you should not relinquish yourself to anything less than what they aspired to, hmm?"

Evangeline nodded, feeling much better than she had when she'd first entered the general store to post her letter to Jennie—much better. Yet she frowned a bit. "The problem is, Mrs.

Perry," she began, lowering her voice, "that the only other available young men in town are my sisters' castoffs." She shrugged, adding, "And none of them really interest me even if they weren't."

"Well, don't you give that another worry, sweet pea," Mrs. Perry reassured, patting the back of Evangeline's hand affectionately. "Some tall drink of water will wander on into town one day. It's always the way it seems . . . least around these parts."

Evangeline watched as Mrs. Perry inked her postmarking stamp and slammed it down on the front of Evangeline's letter to Jennie.

"There we are," she said as she placed the letter to Jennie in a satchel filled with other letters the townsfolk of Meadowlark Lake had written. "Your friend will have her letter in hardly any time at all."

"Thank you, Mrs. Perry," Evangeline said, smiling.

"You're welcome, honey," Mrs. Perry said with a wink. "Now you have yourself a nice afternoon. And tell your sweet stepmamma that I said hello, all right?"

"I will," Evangeline assured the woman.

Stepping out of the general store, Evangeline glanced around in search of her little sister Shay. Shay had been Evangeline's near con-stant companion the past few months—ever since Sheriff Montrose, Judge Ipswich, and Evangeline's newest brother-in-law, Rowdy Gates, had exchanged gunfire with the Morrison brothers' gang of outlaws. It seemed the incident had frightened little Shay Ipswich more than her family had initially realized. Therefore, instead of taking her poor marmalade cat, Molly, for leashed walks on her own, Shay had begun begging Evangeline to accompany her.

"Evie!" Evangeline heard Shay call.

Looking across the street to the diner, Evangeline saw that Shay sat in conversation with Warren Ackerman—a little boy in town just a couple of years older than Shay.

"Warren and me are just sittin' over here talkin'," Shay called. "Is it okay if I stay with Warren a while longer? He says he'll walk home with me and Molly."

Evangeline giggled as she looked down to where Molly sat looking bored but patient at Shay's feet. She shook her head, as ever astonished at the nonsense the poor old marmalade feline put up with.

"Yes, sweetheart," Evangeline called. Her own smile broadened as Shay's dark eyes lit up with delight. "But don't linger too long, all right? Don't let Kizzy and me start worrying about you."

"I won't," Shay assured her older sister.

Evangeline giggled to herself as she watched

14

Warren Ackerman's face pink up with embarrassment when Shay linked her arm with his. It seemed Shay and Warren had been nearly inseparable at times—ever since they'd played the bride and groom in the Tom Thumb wedding presented to the townsfolk that past summer. They'd become fast friends, and Evangeline was glad her littlest sister didn't want for companionship.

Exhaling a heavy sigh, Evangeline turned toward home. "Even my baby sister has a beau," she mumbled to herself.

Inhaling a deep breath of fresh autumn air, however, Evangeline lifted her chin, straightened her posture, and started for home. After all, now that she'd made her decision, she had so much to do in preparing for her trip. First and foremost was telling her family about her plans.

Evangeline wondered how they would feel about it—about her agreeing to Jennie's request that she come and stay with her until the baby was born sometime near the end of October. She wondered if they'd be upset with her for not having discussed it with them before she'd written to Jennie and promised that she would travel out to help her. Certainly she knew that Shay would be disappointed. Yet Calliope and Rowdy lived so close that Shay would never be too lonesome. And Shay did have her friend Warren to keep her company too. Furthermore,

Amoretta and Brake would be moving back to Meadowlark Lake before the snows settled in. So between two older sisters, two brothers-in-law, and her father and mother, Shay would be more than attended to.

Of course, Kizzy was expecting a baby as well, and Evangeline had experienced a measure of guilt about leaving her. Yet Kizzy seemed as robust and as strong as ever. Therefore, Evangeline had little doubt that Kizzy would be fine, and she would have Amoretta and Calliope to watch over her. In any case, Jennie's baby was due near to a month before Kizzy's was. So there would be plenty of time for Evangeline to return home for Thanksgiving and the birth of her new little brother or sister, as well as the Christmas holidays.

Evangeline sighed with self-assurance that going to Jennie was the best venue before her. Jennie needed her help. Her family in Meadowlark Lake did not.

She glanced about then to the beauty of autumn all around her. The trees that dotted the main thoroughfare of Meadowlark Lake were already boasting colorful leaves of crimson and orange and gold. The pumpkins nestled betwixt the vines in the fields on the horizon just beyond town were already a beautiful orange where they lay. No doubt Meadowlark Lake's annual pumpkin parade held on All Hallow's Eve would be a

16

breathtaking sight to behold. At the thought of missing the town's All Hallow's Eve social, a twinge of regret did indeed pinch Evangeline's heart. But Jennie had assured Evangeline that autumn in Red Peak was just as lovely as in any other town out West.

Therefore, she sighed with satisfaction in her decision to visit Jennie and continued to amble toward home.

"You're back already, Evie?" Kizzy asked as Evangeline entered the house through the back kitchen door. "I thought you'd linger awhile with Mrs. Perry."

Evangeline smiled as she studied her striking young stepmother a moment. Pregnancy only complemented Kizzy's dark beauty—only made her dark eyes appear more mysterious and her lovely smile more soothing.

"We chatted for a bit," Evangeline explained. "But for some reason, I just wanted to get home." She added, "And Shay wanted to stay and play with Warren for a little while. I told her it would be fine. I hope you don't mind."

Kizzy giggled, shaking her head with amusement. "Not at all. Shay certainly is sweet on that little boy, isn't she?"

Evangeline laughed a little as well. "She certainly is," she agreed.

Kizzy smiled at Evangeline and suggested, "Why don't you sit down for a bit and keep

17

me company while I finish mixin' this cake for dessert tonight, hmmm?"

"All right," Evangeline agreed. She took a seat at the kitchen table, exhaling a rather weary-sounding sigh as she did so.

Kizzy Ipswich's eyes narrowed as she studied Evangeline. There was a growing unhappiness in Lawson Ipswich's eldest daughter. Kizzy had watched it spread through her countenance for the past six months or so, and she sensed what was causing it—though she did not know how to stop it. She knew *what* would stop it but not how to make the *what* happen.

Evangeline's history was somewhat a sad one. Her mother, Lawson's first wife, had passed away when Evangeline was only twelve. And as nearly always happened in such situations, Evangeline began to be the one to care for her two younger sisters, Amoretta and Calliope. Forced into being a woman with responsibility at such a young age had stripped Evangeline of most of the care-free and pleasurable parts of adolescence and young-womanhood. Furthermore, the loss of her mother and consequent load of responsibility had left its mark on her heart and soul as well.

Of course, Amoretta and Calliope were also devastated by the death of their mother. But they had been younger than Evangeline—still children—and had not borne the brunt of effect that Evangeline had. And now Evangeline sat at the kitchen table, knowing that both her younger sisters had met, fallen in love with, and married astonishingly handsome men who were strong, loving, and thoroughly obsessed with their wives. Even her own father had fallen in love with Kizzy—and, in marrying her, acquired another daughter who was young and fresh and vibrant. And there was the baby on the way—another joy her father would know that Evangeline could not yet imagine herself being blessed with.

Oh, the girl wasn't bitter—not in the least of it—a fact that spoke to Kizzy of Evangeline's high character and strong heart. But a nearly tangible sense of disappointment and heightening unhappiness had begun to settle around her like a veil of lost hope, and it worried Kizzy.

"What's eatin' at your thoughts, Evie?" Kizzy asked then. She chose that moment to finally inquire of Evangeline about her feelings, because the two of them were alone in the house. She knew it would be easier for Evangeline to express concerns or deep feelings then, as opposed to when her father and Shay were present.

Evangeline shrugged. "Oh, nothing so much as is worth discussing now, I don't think."

But Kizzy smiled. "Tell me, Evie. What's in your mind?"

• • •

Evangeline's heart began to race with anxiety as the idea settled in her that perhaps she should confide in Kizzy. After all, Kizzy was a wise woman—far wiser than most women of her young age. By past experience, Evangeline had come to know that it was often very sensible and helpful to confide in Kizzy. Furthermore, it was well Kizzy knew Evangeline's father and how he would feel and react to certain things.

And so in an instant Evangeline decided to leap and said, "I've written Jennie and told her I would travel to be with her until the baby arrives. She's terribly worried, especially now that the doctor has put her to bed for the remainder of her time. I plan to leave next week—to have someone drive me up to Langtree where I can board the train to Red Peak to be with Jennie."

She watched as Kizzy continued to stir the cake batter in the bowl she had propped in one arm. Her heart hammered with trepidation as she waited for Kizzy's response.

Thankfully, Kizzy responded quickly by smiling and saying, "I think it's a wonderful idea, Evie! You need to get away from Meadow-lark Lake for a while, I think. And your friend Jennie . . . well, it sounds like she certainly needs help, not to mention some extra companionship. I imagine it's quite a miserable thing to be put to bed for over a month."

All at once, Evangeline's heart leapt with excitement. "Oh, Kizzy, really? Do you really think I should go? I mean, I've already written to her and told her that I would, but I've been so afraid to tell everyone . . . especially Daddy. But if *you* think it's wise for me to go, then all my fears will be settled."

Kizzy smiled and nodded her reassurance as she said, "I *do* think you should go, Evie. There's nothing here for you at the moment. You need an adventure of sorts. And though I do admit some concern over the fact that you will be servin' someone again—for it seems you've done that at every turn—I do think you need somethin' different for now." Kizzy paused, quirked one eyebrow, and added, "Now as for your father— mind you, he might not be as sure as I am that you need to go, but I'll explain things to him, and he'll come around. So no worries there. Though I do think you should talk to him right away about it."

"Oh, I will!" Evangeline exclaimed. The joy at knowing Kizzy approved of her decision sparked sheer delight in her at the prospect of leaving Meadowlark Lake for a while and seeing Jennie again. "We were such good friends as girls, Jennie and I," Evangeline told Kizzy. "The fun we used to have!" She giggled and added, "And the mischief we used to get into! I think we must've driven our mothers nearly mad with our antics." She sighed, saddened at the memory of the loss of her mother. "Of course, that was before . . . before . . ."

"Before your mother passed away and you stepped into the responsibilities left by her absence," Kizzy finished.

"Yes," Evangeline admitted. Quickly, however, she countered, "Not that I minded at all, Kizzy . . . truly! I loved caring for Amoretta and Calliope. It's just that . . . well, I miss being young and carefree the way Jennie and I were when we were children."

"Well, you're still very young, Evangeline Ipswich," Kizzy reminded.

But Evangeline countered, "I'm old enough that Floyd Longfellow thinks I'd make a good mother for his little girls."

Kizzy rolled her eyes and laughed. "Ha! Floyd Longfellow doesn't care about you being a mother for his girls. He's just smitten by your youth and beauty, Evangeline. The motherin' of his girls is the last thing on his mind where you're concerned." Kizzy shook her head and said, "And besides, once you're gone off to Red Peak to Jennie, Floyd will start pantin' over Blanche Gardener, Winnie Montrose, or some other pretty young thing in town. So don't let the fact that an older man is sweet on you start you to thinkin' you're too old for the likes of the young bucks." Kizzy smiled and winked at Evangeline.

"But I will tell you this," she began. "When the day comes that one of them young bucks comes along and captures your attention, Evie . . . you're gonna need to let him know he's got it."

"What do you mean?" Evangeline asked—for she was a bit confused by Kizzy's instruction.

"I mean that you're a unique beauty, my darlin'," Kizzy explained, "the kind of beauty that good, humble men are afraid to pursue."

But Evangeline sighed with disagreement. "Now I *know* you and Daddy have been talking about me . . . because that's what he always tells me."

"Well, he tells you that because it's the truth," Kizzy said. "Men of good character and heroic hearts tend to have very humble souls, Evie. They tend toward thinkin' they're not good enough for a raven-haired beauty with deep emerald eyes and a name like Evangeline Ipswich."

Evangeline giggled and shook her head with amusement. "A raven-haired beauty with deep emerald eyes, am I?"

"Yes. You are," Kizzy confirmed. She inhaled a breath of determination and continued, "For instance, your newest brother-in-law . . . how long did he pine away after your sister Calliope, thinkin' he wasn't worthy of her, hmm? A long time, I think. And it's worse with you, because your features are dark and mysterious. It intimidates some men."

23

As Evangeline's deep emerald eyes met Kizzy's deep brown ones, she suddenly understood what Kizzy was expressing. "You're speaking from your own experience, I would guess," she offered.

"Yes," Kizzy answered, "though I never saw myself as some great beauty—or even a simple beauty. Pshaw, I always said. I think it was merely that I'm dark-haired and dark-eyed, with gypsy blood in my veins that the sort of men I was attracted to never approached me. Still, your father argues otherwise with me." Kizzy smiled, blushed a little, and almost whispered, "But your father wasn't afraid of me . . . not in any regard." Quickly she added, "Yet I *did* have to encourage him for some reason. And that's why I'm tellin' you, Evie. When there finally arrives a man that captures your eye—and therefore your heart—you must give confidence to him. Let him know that you're wantin' his attention."

Evangeline mulled over what Kizzy had told her, but only for an instant before she said, "Well, that's neither here nor there anyway. I'm going up to be with Jennie. And besides, I'm sure there are even fewer eligible young men in Red Peak than there are here in Meadowlark Lake." Evangeline frowned, shook her head, and waved a hand as if dismissing her thoughts. "I need to go to Jennie. That's why I'm going."

"I know," Kizzy said.

Her voice was calming, and Evangeline returned to her feelings of excitement about going to be with Jennie.

"Just do tell your father soon, all right, Evangeline?" Kizzy asked in an almost pleading manner. "You're his eldest daughter, honey. You'll be the one he has the hardest time lettin' go."

Evangeline smiled, again amazed at Kizzy's insight. "I won't wait, Kizzy. I'll tell him tonight . . . just after dinner."

Kizzy nodded and said, "Thank you, Evie." She giggled then, exclaiming, "Oh, I'm so excited for you! What an adventure it will be, hmm?"

Evangeline laughed at Kizzy's obvious delight in Evangeline's pending trip. For a moment, she wasn't too certain how traveling to help care for a bedridden woman qualified as an adventure, but the more she thought about it as an adventure, the more it felt as if it would be.

Yes, throughout the remainder of the day, Evangeline thought of traveling on the train from Langtree to Red Peak—of seeing the beautiful red rock Jennie had told her composed the hills and mesas around the town, of witnessing so much in a place she'd never been before. And most adventurous of all would be the time spent with Jennie. If the delight and exuberance in Jennie's letters to Evangeline indicated how thoroughly she had remained the same

25

mischievous, amusing person she had been as a girl, then Evangeline knew that her trip north to see her friend would indeed be the adventure of a lifetime!

CHAPTER TWO

She'd been so sure! Evangeline had been so certain, so confident in her decision to travel to Red Peak to be with Jennie. Yet now as she heard the conductor call, "All aboard!"—as she clung to her father, feeling an unfamiliar agony at the realization she would be parted from him for the first time in all her life—she wasn't so unwavering in her determination to see Jennie through her difficult time as she had been even the day before.

"Daddy?" she whispered, inhaling the comforting scent of his shaving soap as she clung tightly to him. She buried her face against his neck just as she'd done as a child. "Daddy, I'm not sure . . ."

"Of course you're not sure, sweet pea," Lawson Ipswich soothed. The low, reassuring intonation of his voice did serve to calm Evangeline—if only a little. "No one's ever sure when they leave home for their first trip away from their family. But this will be good for you, Evie—an adventure of one type or another. I'm certain of it. And I know that being with Jennie again will give you a sense of liberation of sorts— –something you haven't known in a very long time."

Lawson sighed, holding his daughter at arm's

length as he studied her. Even for his strong reassurances, Evangeline could see the emotion in his eyes—the sadness and anxiety. Oh, his words were telling her she should go to Jennie, but his heart was telling *him* otherwise.

"And besides, it's not forever, after all," Lawson added, forcing a smile. "It's just a month or so, and then you'll be back with us again." Lawson released Evangeline, somewhat unwillingly, and turned to Brake McClendon, his son-in-law. "And by the time you get back, Brake and I will have moved he and Amoretta back to Meadowlark Lake, and we'll, all of us, spend Thanksgiving and Christmas Day together, hmm?"

"That's right," Brake agreed, adding a reassuring smile of his own. "We'll miss you, Evangeline," he assured her.

Evangeline smiled. Her sister, Amoretta, gave Evangeline one last hug and then turned to melt into the strong embrace of her husband, Brake.

"You'll be back to us soon enough, won't you, Evie?" Amoretta more stated than asked.

"Of course, darling," Evangeline answered, brushing more tears from her cheeks.

"Last call! All aboard!" the conductor shouted again.

The loud huffing and puffing of the train's powerful steam engine as it came to life did nothing to settle Evangeline's anxiety as she

28

turned and quickly boarded the train car behind her.

As the train slowly began to pull away from the Langtree station, Amoretta kissed her own hand, tossing the invisible token of affection to Evangeline. Brake waved, as well as her father. Evangeline thought she'd never seen him look so sad—at least, not since the death of her mother. Furthermore, her own heart was aching so thoroughly that the instant was painful to endure.

What was she thinking in leaving her family? Even for such a short time, and for such a very good reason?

For a moment, Evangeline considered dashing to the back of the train car and jumping off the train. But as the train began to gather more speed, and as she remembered her traveling trunk that was in the storage car, she closed her eyes and reached deep inside her soul to find her courage. Jennie needed her—truly needed her. Whether it was physical help in keeping house and cooking meals or company and encouragement, Jennie did *need* Evangeline. She wasn't needed at home— at least not in the same way Jennie needed her. Her father had Kizzy and Shay to love and look after—not to mention a new baby on the way. Her younger sisters, Amoretta and Calliope, each had husbands who were in need of them. And though Evangeline knew her family loved her and needed her presence to make them feel complete,

Jennie needed her company and encouragement more.

Evangeline thought of all these reasons over and over again as the train traveled north, leaving her family farther and farther behind. Gradually, she found that her tears diminished and then stopped. She began to think of Jennie and the tender friendship they'd enjoyed as girls. Thus, also gradually, Evangeline's heart began to lighten as she thought of seeing Jennie again— of talking with her, laughing with her, and being near to help her in her time of distress and need.

Exhaling a heavy sigh—the sigh borne of weathering an emotional good-bye and next realizing that she was indeed excited at the prospect of venturing to something out of the ordinary—Evangeline began to gaze out the train car window at the brilliant colors with which autumn was adorning the landscape.

Crimson and orange sumac, golden cotton-wood, and scarlet maple mingled in harmony with evergreen to line the landscape along the railroad tracks as the train traveled. Creek banks were lined with cattails, some already beginning to burst into silky white tufts that the wind would capture and carry to seed new venues.

Now and again, the train would travel past the outskirts of some small town. There farmers were harvesting pumpkins in fields of withered vines near vast acres of cornstalks, which now stood drab and yellowed in sleeping—spent by a healthy harvest. Shabby scarecrows, once hearty sentinels of summer, lingered in worn, sun-blanched clothes, looking tired yet happy to know winter would bring them rest.

In truth, Evangeline had not traveled along a more beautiful venue, and it cheered her. Slowly, her anxiety over leaving her family home began to lessen, and her enthusiasm at seeing Jennie returned.

Evangeline rested her head against the back of her seat and closed her eyes. She smiled as she thought back on the joy she and Jennie had known in each other's company as young girls— the days of sunshine and making daisy chains, of tea parties in her mother's parlor, and of chilled autumn ghost hunts in the old cemeteries that dotted the historic venues of Boston. Those had been carefree days indeed—days spent in playtime and dreaming, in giggling and sharing secrets with Jennie. Of course that had all been before Evangeline's mother and baby brother had died—before Evangeline had had to, at the tender age of twelve, step into her mother's shoes to care for her two young sisters, Amoretta and Calliope. It had been before Jennie's older brother had up and left his home and family one day, leaving Jennie distraught and Evangeline secretly heartbroken. It had been before Jennie had married Calvin McKee and moved west—

before Evangeline's own father had decided to leave Boston himself, thereby moving Evangeline and her two sisters west as well, to the town of Meadowlark Lake.

In truth, those young years of Evangeline's life spent in the blissful comfort of family and the cherished friendship of Jennie seemed so very long ago. Evangeline knew she was different now than she had been—and not just grown up. Evangeline knew she was somewhat weathered by tragedy and emotional hardship. Therefore, the prospect of seeing Jennie again began to seem like a dream—an escape to a thread from the past—and for a moment, Evangeline wondered if perhaps, in seeing Jennie again, she might regain a small measure of the carefree happiness she had lost when her mother had died.

Still, she knew it was best not to expect too much joviality in Jennie's company. After all, Jennie was in a bad way, bedridden until her baby arrived. Furthermore, she had a husband, and no doubt Calvin would require the majority of Jennie's attention and companionship.

Opening her eyes once more, Evangeline determined, however, that even though her visit to Red Peak would require a lot of work in keeping house and making meals for Jennie and her husband, she would find the time for reminiscing, laughing, and sharing secrets with her old friend. And maybe, just maybe, doing so would help

Evangeline regain a measure of the person she might have been—before loss, heartache, and responsibility had put her on a different track in life. Perhaps her adventure to visit Jennie would work a bit like the railway switch Evangeline could see the train turning onto in that very moment. And then perhaps Evangeline wouldn't feel quite so alone so much of the time. Perhaps she wouldn't find herself longing for something that was missing in her—something that she couldn't even identify to herself.

Evangeline smiled as her heart lightened. Yes! She was glad she was taking the trip to see Jennie, for she felt as if some sort of wild exhilaration that had been long suppressed had been restored to her.

Gazing out the window again, Evangeline sighed. She had made the right decision in going to visit Jennie. She did wince a moment when she thought of the note from Shay she carried in her pocket—a note moist with tears and verbose with descriptions of how her little sister would miss Evangeline. Still, she choked back her emotions of missing her family and thought only of the visit ahead. Her father had been right: Evangeline did feel a sense of liberation, and this before she'd even reached the destination!

CHAPTER THREE

As she stepped off the train and onto the Red Peak train platform, Evangeline shivered a little, for the weather was considerably colder than it had been in Langtree. Certainly autumn was brilliant in its October glory when she'd left Meadowlark Lake earlier that same day. Yet cool and crisp as the morning air had been in Langtree, the early evening atmosphere of Red Peak was nigh unto frigid.

"Here you go, miss," the tall, rather elderly porter said as he set her traveling trunk down on the platform next to her. "You enjoy your visit now."

"Thank you," Evangeline said, smiling as the porter tipped his hat to her and accepted the coins of gratuity she offered.

"Thank you, miss," the man said as he shuffled off to board the train once more.

Evangeline inhaled a deep breath of cold autumn air. Glancing about for a moment, she was not the least bit disappointed with the pines and gold-leafed aspens that surrounded the train station. Quite the opposite of Meadowlark Lake and Langtree's crimson maples and flaming orange and scarlet sumac, the deep richness of the evergreens mingled with the quivering yellow of the aspen leaves was just as beautiful—simply different.

Evangeline startled a little as a somewhat quiet bark drew her attention from the autumn vista before her and to a medium-sized brown dog that had suddenly appeared at her side. The dog stood panting happily, as if he'd known her all her life, and it quite warmed Evangeline's heart.

"Well, aren't you a friendly little fellow?" she giggled as the dog—who she quickly noticed was missing one hind leg—sat at her feet, wagging its tail and panting in happy anticipation of attention.

Again Evangeline giggled. "Aren't you just a handsome man? Yes, you are," she said to the dog as she hunkered down and scratched behind his ears. She laughed when the dog's one hind leg began to beat the train platform as a signal of delight. "Oh, you *are* a sweetheart, aren't you? I bet you're quite the Romeo in town too, hmmm?"

"Well, well, well. If it isn't Evangeline Ipswich," came a man's voice from behind her. "And I see you've already won over Jones."

Evangeline felt goose bumps break over her entire body, for she'd instantly recognized the voice, even for the near six years it had been since she'd last heard it.

Rendered breathless by the familiar, yet long absent, sensation of excitement that washed over her, Evangeline felt a nervous trembling begin in her bosom as she slowly stood and turned around. A quiet gasp escaped her as she gazed up into the indecently handsome face of Jennie's elder brother, Hutchner LaMontagne.

"H-Hutch?" Evangeline stammered as she continued to stare at him. As cute as Hutchner LaMontagne had been as a boy—as exceptionally good-looking as he'd been as a very young man—it was all nothing compared with the magnificent specimen of manly attractiveness that full-grown manhood had bestowed upon him.

Evangeline quickly surmised Hutch was much taller even than he had been when she'd last seen him—even taller than her father. His shoulders were broader than broad, as was the expanse of his chest. Where it showed beneath his hat, it was obvious that his hair was still the same dark, warm brown that had ever lingered in Evangeline's reminiscent daydreams. Likewise his eyes were the same familiar, breathtaking, riveting blue. Yet his jaw was more squared, all the more pronounced and complemented by a few days of dark whisker growth. His nose was as straight as ever and his smile even more captivating than it had been.

"Oh, good, you remember me then, huh?" Hutch asked, smiling his alluring smile at her.

"Of-of course," Evangeline managed. She unconsciously took a step backward, for he unsettled her—just as he always had.

Evangeline gasped, however, as, when she began to take another step backward, she found that there was no flooring directly beneath her, and she began to stumble.

"Careful now, darlin'," Hutch said as he reached out, caught hold of her arms, steadied her, and pulled her forward a step or two. "Jennie would skin me alive if I brought you home all banged up." He chuckled as he continued to smile at her, and Evangeline's heart leapt in her chest at the familiar and once very beloved sound.

"Wh-what are you doing here, Hutch?" Evangeline asked. She was more than entirely astounded; she was nearly in a state of shock! For the fact of the matter was, since she'd been a little girl—in truth, as far back as her first memory of life—she'd been in love with Jennie's older brother, Hutchner. The fact that six years previously, he'd up and left Boston to find his way out West—and unknowingly broken her heart in doing so—hadn't changed the effect his presence had on her one whit. Goose bumps had broken over her arms when he'd reached out to steady her. His fixed sapphire eyes caused her heart to quiver and her limbs to tremble.

"What?" he asked, quirking one handsome brow. "Aren't you glad to see me again? After all, it's been six years, hasn't it? Did you give me up as a friend so fast as that?" He winked one of his delicious, teasing winks.

"Of c-course not," Evangeline managed. "It's just that . . . well, you surprised me so. Jennie didn't mention that you would be here too. I'm just surprised, that's all."

"Well, that's sure good to hear," he said. "I swear, you went pale as a ghost when you saw me. I almost laughed because you looked so shocked. But I didn't want you to faint or something and topple down on top of ol' Jones." Hutch reached down and scratched the brown dog behind one ear. "He's already down one leg, you see. I wouldn't want him to break another. Otherwise I might have to take to carrying him everywhere." He laughed, looked to Evangeline, and asked, "Remember those old Bostonian ladies we used to make fun of? The ones that carried their little dogs around or kept them on their laps?"

"Of course," Evangeline assured him. She smiled at the memory.

There was silence between them a moment—an awkward silence as Hutch seemed to study Evangeline from head to toe for a time.

"Well, I guess I better get you to Jennie's place," Hutch said. "I'm sure she'll be chomping at the bit to start catching up on things with you." He turned, looked at her traveling trunk, and asked, "Is this all you've got?"

"Yes," Evangeline assured him with a nod.

Her eyes widened as he turned, picked up her

trunk, and easily hefted it onto one shoulder. He was so intimidating in his height and visible musculature. He wore a pair of worn boots with his trousers legs tucked into them, a blue shirt, and suspenders. Evangeline thought how differently he was dressed than the last time she'd seen him in Boston—at a wedding, dressed in his formal attire. A slight smile curled her lips as she realized she preferred his present togs.

"Come on, Jones," he called to his dog. The dog hopped up and very ably began walking in front of his master—toward a wagon and team of horses that Hutch nodded toward.

"That's my rig, there," he said. "Ma'am," he added, tipping his hat to her and nodding to indicate she should proceed before him.

Evangeline smiled and said, "I see you still have your city manners."

"Nope," Hutch said, however. "I swapped them for some country ones. I find they're not as stiff and serious."

Still smiling, Evangeline did precede him, following the happily panting Jones to the wagon.

Once Hutch had deposited her traveling trunk into the wagon bed, he offered her his hand to assist her in climbing up onto the wagon's seat.

"Ma'am," he said, again.

"Thank you," Evangeline said, accepting his assistance. Of course, instantly she wished she hadn't—for her hand where he held it so instantly warmed with the excitement of his touch that it began to tremble again.

Hoping he hadn't noticed her nervous reaction to him, Evangeline settled herself on the wagon seat, smoothing the skirt of her dress and straightening her posture.

Hutch whistled to Jones, and Evangeline was amazed at how nimbly the three-legged dog leapt up onto the wagon. She laughed when Jones plopped his hindquarters on the wagon seat between she and Hutch and rested his head in her lap.

"He's very friendly," Evangeline said as she softly patted the dog's head and scratched behind his ears.

"Only to pretty girls," Hutch said, winking at her. He shrugged, adding, "And to me, of course."

Evangeline felt the heat of a blush rise to her cheeks. Six years had passed—six long years—and yet Hutch's implication that she was a "pretty girl" still made her blush and feel tingly inside. She wasn't sixteen anymore, and she hadn't seen Hutch for years and years. Therefore, Evangeline was fairly confounded at why he still affected her so.

In fact, he was probably married! That thought instantly depressed her. She glanced to his left hand to see if he wore a wedding ring. He did

41

not. But that didn't mean he wasn't married. Many men didn't wear wedding rings.

"What're you looking at?" he asked unexpectedly.

Evangeline's muscles tensed. She couldn't tell him she'd been checking to see if he wore a wedding ring.

Therefore, finding the courage to look up at him and meet his curious gaze, she answered, "Y-you're very tall. Much taller than I remember."

Hutch chuckled with amusement and slapped the lines at his team's backs. As the wagon lurched forward, he said, "Well, you're very beautiful." He looked back to her. "Even more beautiful than I remember."

Again Evangeline blushed. She glanced away from Hutch, down to the dog still resting his head in her lap.

"I see you haven't lost your charm," she said.

"And I see that you haven't lost your humility," he countered with an approving grin.

Evangeline's blush deepened. She was flustered, wondering why he unsettled her so entirely. Oh, certainly, most of her childhood and adolescence she'd often dreamt about riding in a carriage or buggy with the handsome and dashing Hutch LaMontagne at the reins, but those were silly dreams from long ago. Therefore, she was awed at her own weakness—her vulnerability to

42

the wiles of a man she hadn't seen in six years.

"So," Hutch began, "Jennie tells me you're still not married."

If Evangeline were uncomfortable in Hutch's presence a moment before, now she was nigh unto distressed!

"Um . . . that's correct," she said. "That's me—the old spinster of the Ipswich family," she rather grumbled with embarrassment.

But Hutch looked at her with surprise. "Spinster?" he asked. "Oh, I'd hardly think that you would qualify as a spinster. How old are you now? Twenty?"

"Twenty-two," Evangeline admitted, disheartened.

"Twenty-two?" Hutch exclaimed. "Why, you're still a baby! I can't believe you're even wearing long skirts. Seems to me you should still be in pigtails."

Evangeline shook her head and smiled. "And there it is . . . that Hutchner LaMontagne charm."

"Well, I don't know about charm," he continued. "But if you're walking around thinking you're a spinster at twenty-two, what does that make me—still a bachelor at twenty-six?"

He wasn't married! He still wasn't married! The knowledge caused far, far more excitement and delight to bubble up inside Evangeline's bosom than she felt it should have.

"An old rake, I suppose," she teased.

"An old rake?" Hutch asked, looking at her and wearing an expression of deep concern.

"Oh, of course not," Evangeline assured him. "I was just teasing you. And anyway, it's perfectly acceptable for a man not to be married at a young age. In fact, my father's wife is only a few years older than I am, and no one even thinks it's strange. But a woman not being married by the time she's twenty-two . . . well, most of society frowns on that."

"Well, that's just foolish," Hutch commented. "As I said, I'm surprised you're even wearing long skirts yet."

Evangeline smiled, feeling the same tender-hearted warmth toward Hutch and his kindness as ever she had as a young girl.

"In fact, I wasn't all for it as easily as you might think when Calvin up and proposed to Jennie, you know," Hutch offered.

Evangeline was somewhat taken aback by the revelation—but only for a moment, as then she remembered just how protective Hutch had always been of his little sister. Still, for the sake of her own interest, she asked, "You weren't?"

Hutch shook his head. "Nope. I thought she was too young, too inexperienced in life. And she hadn't known Calvin more than a month or two either." He shrugged, exhaled a rather guilty sounding sigh, and continued. "In fact, it's why they're out here in Red Peak. After our parents died, Jennie stayed with our aunt and uncle in Boston. She met Calvin, and he sent me a telegram asking my permission to marry her. As I said, I wasn't too keen on the idea, so I had him come out here and work with me at the livery for several weeks before I would agree to their marriage." He paused, looked to Evangeline, and explained, "I just felt I needed to look out for her, you know? I felt bad for not going back to Boston right away when our folks passed."

Evangeline smiled with encouragement. "You're a wise man, and a good and protective brother."

"Well, I hope so," he said. "Fortunately, Calvin understood and came out just as I asked him to. In fact, he liked it so much here, he asked Jennie if she'd be willing to come out, and she was. I figured a man who was willing to go through everything he did in putting up with my shenanigans was a good man indeed." He shrugged. "So Jennie married Calvin right here in Red Peak. And they've lived here ever since. They live just a few houses down from mine."

"And does Calvin still work with you at the livery?" Evangeline asked.

Hutch shook his head. "Nope. He works over at the lumber mill. He seems happier over there, being that there's a bit more to keep a man busy."

"Well, I can tell that Jennie is very happy with Calvin," Evangeline sighed. "It's obvious in the way she talks about him in her letters."

"They do love each other more than most married couples I've ever seen." Hutch grinned. "It makes me feel comforted to know she's happy and taken care of." He turned and looked to Evangeline, asking, "Now what's this about your daddy marrying a much younger woman? Just older than you, you say?"

Evangeline smiled and nodded. "Yes . . . Kizzy," she answered. "She's beautiful! A gypsy, in fact, and she had a little girl already, my new little sister, Shay. She's just as beautiful as her mother and keeps us in stitches with her amusing antics. Furthermore, Kizzy's expecting a baby herself, due to arrive about Thanksgiving."

Hutch smiled and chuckled. "Well, good for the judge!" he exclaimed.

"I have photographs that I brought with me to show to Jennie," Evangeline continued. "Photographs of everyone in the family. So since you're here, you can see them too!"

"I look forward to it," he said. He paused a moment and then asked, "I take it by your astonishment in seeing me at the train station that my little sister didn't tell you I lived in Red Peak too, hmm?"

Again Evangeline blushed. Shaking her head, she admitted, "No, she didn't mention it."

Hutch's handsome brow puckered. "I wonder why not?" he asked. Then answering his own question, he added, "She probably thought I'd scare you off, that you wouldn't want to come visit if you knew her old rake of a brother was in town."

Hutch winked at Evangeline, and she giggled. "Maybe," she teased. "But I know a few old rakes, and you're not one of them."

"Jennie did tell me that there's some old man pursuing you in . . . is it Meadowlark Lake?" he said.

"Meadowlark Lake, yes," Evangeline confirmed.

"Jennie says he's a poet or some such thing?" Hutch prodded.

Evangeline smiled. "His name is Mr. Longfellow, and he's a farmer, not a poet. And I know you well enough to know you're just being a smart aleck, Hutchner LaMontagne."

He grinned and shrugged with being guilty as accused. "Are you gonna marry him?" he asked.

"Heavens no!" Evangeline exclaimed, blushing. "He's old enough to be my father!"

"But you just said your father married a woman hardly older than you," Hutch baited.

"Well, that is entirely different! My father is an entirely different sort of man than Mr. Longfellow," Evangeline defended. "And besides, I don't find poor Mr. Longfellow at all attractive.

And he never laughs . . . rarely speaks for that matter!"

"Whoa, Nelly!" Hutch laughed. "I was just trying to ruffle your feathers, Evie. Jennie already told me you're not interested in the least in the old poet."

Evangeline inhaled a deep breath to calm her temperament. Exhaling a heavy sigh and remembering what a tease Hutch could be, she said, "I see you still like to endeavor to unsettle people."

Hutch's grin broadened. "Oh, and you were always a fun one to unsettle," he said. "It didn't take much, as I recall, to set your bloomers to ruffling."

Evangeline smiled as memories of Hutch's teasing her flooded her mind. "No, it didn't take much. At least not for you."

"Well, it's good to know that you remember me for something, at least," Hutch chuckled.

Remembered him for something? That was certainly understating things. Evangeline remembered Hutch for everything! Sure, his teasing, playful manner was one of the things she remembered most—one of the things she'd always, always loved about her best friend's older brother—but there was so much more than that! Evangeline remembered how friendly he always was to everyone, including her. She thought of how heroic he was—of the time she'd lost her way in the city when she was six years old, having gotten separated from her mother in a crowd, and an eleven-year-old Hutchner LaMontagne finding her—frightened, sobbing, and cold—and carrying her all the way home. She remembered how strong he'd always been, bruising the cheeks and chins of school bullies when they bothered anyone who was too small or afraid to defend themselves. And she thought of the daydreams she had entertained for most of her life until he'd left Boston—daydreams of moments like she was living that very day—daydreams of having Hutch's attention all to herself for a time.

"And here we are," Hutch said as the team turned onto the main thoroughfare of Red Peak. "Jennie and Calvin's house is the one down a ways, the one with the yellow shutters."

He pointed toward a pretty little white house with yellow shutters at the windows. There was a large maple tree in the front yard, whose crimson leaves were already blanketing the ground.

"Oh, it's so warm and inviting!" Evangeline exclaimed aloud.

"Well, Jennie lives there," Hutch said. "What else would you expect?"

Evangeline glanced to him, nodding in agreement. Jennie herself was always warm and inviting. People had always been drawn to Jennie, just like bees to pollen.

Hutch pulled the team to a stop before the welcoming, quaint little house. He leapt down from the wagon seat, followed by Jones, and walked around to assist Evangeline.

"Here," he said, holding out his strong-looking hands to her. "Come on down, and we'll go in. Then I'll come back for your trunk, all right? Jennie's probably ready to fly around the room with impatience."

Placing her hands on Hutch's broad shoulders, Evangeline quivered with delight as his hands went round her waist and he lifted her down from the wagon seat.

"There you are, little Miss Ipswich," he said, smiling at her. "Safely delivered to Red Peak and my sister. No doubt you two will be cackling like hens over old memories in no time."

He offered her his arm, and she accepted it, causing goose bumps to race over her arms and legs. She was being escorted by Hutchner LaMontagne! There had been a time in Boston when every eligible young woman dreamt of just this very pleasure.

Hutch opened the front door to Jennie's house, stepped in, and called, "Oh, baby sister, I have something for you."

"Ahhhh!" came a squeal of delight from a room to one side of the entryway. "Come in here, Evie—this instant! I can't wait one more moment to set eyes on you!"

Evangeline looked up to Hutch, saying, "Thank you so much for coming to get me, Hutch."

Hutch smiled at her, touched the brim of his hat, and said, "My pleasure." He chuckled when Jennie squealed her impatience again and said, "I'll fetch your trunk and put it in the back room where you'll be staying. Tell Jennie I'll be back to help Calvin with supper when I'm finished up at the livery."

"Oh, you don't need to fix supper," Evangeline assured him. "That's what I'm here for." She smiled and, hoping beyond hope that he would agree, said, "Why don't you just come over for supper? About six, all right? I'm sure Calvin would enjoy the company of another man when there are two silly, cackling girls in the bedroom."

Hutch nodded, grinned, and said, "Thank you. I'll be here." Again Jennie squealed. Hutch shook his head with amusement and said, "You better get in there before she gets out of bed and comes racing in here to get you."

Evangeline smiled, nodded, and again said, "Thank you, Hutch." She let go of his arm then, feeling disappointed in knowing he was leaving.

But when next she heard Jennie call, "Evie! Get your fanny in here! I've been waiting all day to see you," she smiled at Hutch and hurried toward the bedroom he nodded toward.

"You girls have fun now," Hutch said as he left by way of the front door.

Evangeline stepped into the bedroom to see her dear friend sitting upright in bed, arms outstretched toward her.

"Evie! Oh, Evie, I am so happy you're here!" Jennie exclaimed.

Evangeline giggled, hurrying to the bed and throwing her arms around Jennie's neck. "I'm so glad I'm here too!" Evangeline exclaimed as they embraced for a long time. She could hear Jennie sniffling and felt her tears on her cheek mingle with her own tears of joy.

"Oh, you're just so beautiful!" Jennie breathed as she held Evangeline's face between her hands and studied her a moment. "More beautiful than even I remember!"

Evangeline shook her head, however, saying, "But look at you! Your hair is so much darker than when we were girls, and your cheeks are so rosy. Expecting a baby makes you all the more radiant."

"And fat!" Jennie giggled. "I swear I feel like an overripe watermelon."

"Well, you don't look like one," Evangeline assured her friend. She studied Jennie's dark brown hair, brown eyes, and rosy cheeks. "You look resplendent! And I'm so glad you asked me to come."

"I'm glad you came, Evie," Jennie said,

brushing a tear from her cheek. "More glad than you even know. I've been having a hard time of it, you see."

As more tears ran over Jennie's cheeks—tears of fear, fatigue, and thankfulness at having a friend close by, Evangeline clasped her hands tightly in her own and said, "Well, I'm here now. And I'm going to take very good care of you, and we'll talk and reminisce and have a wonderful time while we wait for your little bundle to arrive."

"Thank you so much, Evie," Jennie said as she burst into sobbing. "Thank you!"

Evangeline gathered her cherished friend into her arms, consoling her by stroking her hair and telling her that all would be well.

Evangeline was glad she had come. All her anxieties over leaving her family behind washed away in that moment. She knew they would return, but Jennie needed her now— needed her far more than anyone at home did. And if anything in life was certain, it was that Evangeline Ipswich needed to be needed.

CHAPTER FOUR

"Oh, I just keep pinching myself to make sure I'm awake and that you're really here, Evie!" Jennie exclaimed.

Red Peak's doctor, Doctor Swayze, had indeed given Jennie strict instructions for bed rest. However, Jennie explained to Evangeline that she could be out of bed for about an hour or so a day, provided she didn't stay on her feet too long. Therefore, as Evangeline busily prepared supper that evening, Jennie sat on a kitchen chair visiting with her as she did.

"Well, I'm just glad I arrived in time to make some supper for you and Calvin tonight," Evangeline said. "After the stories you've told me about Calvin and Hutch feeding you nothing but bacon and eggs three meals a day—goodness sakes! You must be starving for something else!"

Jennie laughed. "In truth, I never thought a body could get tired of eating bacon. But I am! Still, it was either that or jerky, so I guess I should be thankful that the boys knew how to cook *something!*"

Evangeline giggled at the thought of Hutch trying to make supper for his sister. She hadn't met Jennie's husband, Calvin, yet, but she figured it must be quite a sight to see two men trying to provide three good meals a day for an ailing woman.

"I guess you should be, at that," Evangeline agreed.

She slid a pan of biscuits into the oven, stirred the chicken stew in the big pot on the stove, and said, "And tomorrow I'll bake a cake for you, Jennie. You deserve something sweet."

"Well, I don't know if I necessarily deserve it, but it would be heavenly, Evie!" Jennie sighed with excitement. "Just heavenly!"

Evangeline smiled as she sat down in a chair across the kitchen table from Jennie. She was so glad she was able to help her friend—to give her some much-needed female companion-ship, not to mention something to eat besides eggs and bacon. And now that they'd said their emotional hellos and had an hour or so to talk before Evangeline had started the stew cooking for supper, Evangeline couldn't keep from asking the question she'd been wanting to ask Jennie from the moment she'd looked up to see Hutch standing on the platform at the train station.

"Jennie?" she began. "May I ask you some-thing?"

"Of course," Jennie assured her with a smile. "Although I bet I can ask the question for you," Jennie said, smiling with understanding. "You're going to ask me why I didn't tell you in my letters that Hutch lived in Red Peak too, aren't you?"

Evangeline laughed and nodded, confirming, "Yes! That is exactly what I was going to ask."

Jennie still smiled yet shrugged, guiltily. "In truth?"

"Absolutely," Evangeline encouraged with a smile.

"Well, one reason is that . . . well, I was afraid you wouldn't come to visit me if you knew Hutch was close by," she confessed.

Evangeline shook her head in disbelief. "Why ever would you think that, Jennie? You and I were so close as girls in Boston, and ever since we started exchanging letters, I've just realized how much I miss you. Why would you think that Hutch's living here would keep me from you? For pity's sake, that's the most ridiculous thing I've ever heard."

Jennie nodded in agreement. "I know. I know," she admitted. "I suppose it's just because . . . well, you'll understand one day, Evie. Carrying a child just wreaks havoc with a woman's emotions. I just kept thinking about how . . . about how in love you had always been with Hutch when we were younger, and I just thought that you might think you'd feel uncomfortable around him and not come to see me." She reached out, taking Evangeline's hands in her own. "But now I see this is just like old times when you and I used to have so much fun together, and Hutch was just . . . just there once in a while," she explained with excitement. "And besides," she added, lowering her voice, "it used to be so much fun to watch you wriggle when Hutch paid attention to you, and I'm sure I'll find that it still is."

"Jennie LaMontagne McKee!" Evangeline playfully scolded. "What a thing to say!"

But Jennie merely laughed and said, "Oh, I remember how over the moon you were for Hutch," Jennie giggled. "Your cheeks would blush up red as radishes anytime Hutch spoke to you . . . or even glanced at you for that matter!"

In truth, simply revisiting memories of how infatuated she had been with Hutchner LaMontagne made Evangeline blush again in that very moment. "Oh, believe me, I *do* remember," she admitted. "There were times I thought I might just faint dead away when he looked at me."

"That's because you used to hold your breath when he did," Jennie reminded.

Evangeline laughed, "Oh, that's right! I'd forgotten about that. What a ninny I was, fawning over your older brother like he was some dime novel hero or something." Evangeline put her hands to her warm, pinked-up cheeks. "I'm so embarrassed remembering it now! Hutch must've thought I was the silliest girl in Boston."

"Nonsense," Jennie countered. "Hutch was always very fond of you. He thought you were adorable."

"Adorable?" Evangeline giggled, rolling her eyes.

"Yes, adorable," Jennie confirmed. "He once told me that he figured you'd turn out to be a very beautiful woman."

"Oh, did he now?" Evangeline asked skeptically—even though Hutch had told her she was beautiful just that very day on the wagon ride from the train station to Jennie's home.

"Yes, he did," Jennie answered with a firm nod. "And he was right, wasn't he?"

Evangeline sighed and shook her head, brushing aside Jennie's compliment.

"Well, I'll say this," she began then. "As handsome a young man as Hutch was, he's even more attractive now. He's so tall, so broad-shouldered and brawny, with surely as square a chin as I've ever seen on a good-looking man. I could never have imagined that he'd improve on what were already such profound good looks." She paused a moment and then added, "I was quite astonished when he told me he was, as yet, unmarried."

Jennie smiled. "Well, you know Hutchner," she said. "He never settles for second best or convenience the way some people do. Believe me, he could have his choice of women." Jennie shrugged. "But no one has managed to win his heart yet."

"I find that rather hard to believe," Evangeline admitted.

"Me too," Jennie agreed. "But it's true." Jennie cocked her head to one side then, asking, "And how did your Mr. Floyd Longfellow take the news that you were leaving Meadowlark Lake, hmm?"

Evangeline shrugged. "I have no idea. He didn't say a word to me before I left, even when he passed me in the general store the day before I did." She exhaled a heavy sigh of a burden lifted. "And I'm so very, very glad he didn't. He's a kind man of sorts. But he really just wants a wife so that he'll have a mother for his little girls. Furthermore, I'm not at all attracted to him . . . not a bit."

"Good!" Jennie said. "I don't want an old widower with needy children for you as a husband, Evie. I want you to be swept away in passion, romance, and true, true love the way I have been with Calvin."

"My father was an old widower, you know," Evangeline teased her friend.

But Jennie laughed. "Your father is a mythical Greek god of masculinity and beauty, Evie! Oh, I was so in love with your father when I was about five years old that I once told my mother I was going to marry him one day. You can imagine my devastation when my mother told me that Mr. Ipswich was already married to Mrs. Ipswich and that I couldn't marry him myself." Jennie clamped a hand to her breast over her heart. "I was miserable for a week with despair!"

Evangeline laughed yet sympathized, "How tragic, Jennie! I never knew."

"Yes, I was quite overwrought," Jennie admitted. "It wasn't until Mother allowed me to eat an entire dozen cookies that I was able to rally. And therein is my point: your Mr. Longfellow, the sad widower, and your father, the dashing Judge Ipswich, are two different recipes entirely!" Jennie shook her head and emphatically reiterated, "No. I will not allow you to resign yourself to Mr. Longfellow, the poor, needy man. No. You shall have what I have with Calvin. I am certain of it, Evie. So put those thoughts of resignation—of acceptance that you are not meant to have what I and your two sisters have in love and companionship with a husband—completely from your mind."

"And just how do you know what's in my mind?" Evangeline baited, though she knew exactly how Jennie knew what was in her mind: because Jennie knew what was truly in Evangeline's heart, and it was not this Floyd Longfellow.

"I'd rather you married his son than him! He, at least, sounds as if he has a sense of humor."

Evangeline smiled. "You *do* remember everything in our letters, don't you?"

"Yes, I do!" Jennie assured her. "Especially being that I've had nothing to do for weeks but

61

read them over and over and over while I've lain in bed like an invalid."

"Speaking of which," Evangeline began, rising from her chair, "we best get you back in bed before your husband comes home and thinks I'm not taking proper care of you."

"Oh, Calvin is going to be so glad to have you here, Evie," Jennie said as Evangeline helped her stand. "He hasn't complained—not one word— but I know he must be tired of waiting on me hand and foot, of eating bacon and eggs all the time. After a long day at the lumber mill, he comes home so tired, and I've felt so bad that I haven't been able to do anything for him."

"Well, I hope that I'm worth the inconvenience of having a houseguest," Evangeline said.

"It's no inconvenience, Evie," Jennie said, smiling at her as they walked slowly back to the bedroom. "You're a blessing . . . truly a blessing."

Just as Evangeline had tucked Jennie back into bed, the front door burst open, and a stocky, solid-looking man with light blond hair and blue eyes entered the house.

"Jennie?" Calvin McKee called as he entered the bedroom. The man immediately removed his hat and lunged toward the bed. Without so much as a word to Evangeline, Calvin began kissing his wife in quite a passionate manner. "How are you, honey? Are you feeling okay? Did you stay off your feet today?"

Jennie giggled, kissed Calvin squarely on the mouth, and answered, "I'm fine, Cal. I'm fine. And I'm all the better now that Evangeline has arrived."

Calvin stood then, turned to Evangeline, and offered her his hand. "Calvin McKee, Miss Evangeline," he said.

His handshake was so firm and strong, Evangeline felt it all the way to her bones.

"It's so nice to meet you at last, Mr. McKee," Evangeline greeted him. "And thank you so much for allowing me to come and visit."

"Oh, you call me Calvin, Miss Evangeline," Calvin chuckled. His blue eyes lit up like stars, and something about the bright sincerity of his smile made Evangeline giggle a little. "And we're just so glad you were willing to come all the way up to Red Peak! I've had to work so much at the mill, and I worry so about my Jennie. It will ease my mind like you'll never know to have you here to care for her when I'm away." He paused a moment, sniffed the air, closed his eyes, and sighed, "Do I smell stew and biscuits?"

Evangeline laughed. "Yes, you do! In fact, I best see to the biscuits before they burn right through."

Calvin sighed once more, again sniffing the air. "I never thought I'd say this, but it is so nice to smell something other than bacon cooking in the house."

Evangeline, startling her from her reminis-
cences.

"I'd expect nothing else!" Evangeline
exclaimed. She was pleased with the way
Calvin was so attentive to Jennie.

She smiled up at Hutch, momentarily mesmerized and unable to move by his purely
alluring presence.

He grinned and asked, "You don't mind if I join
you in here, do you?"

"Of course not," she assured him. "I'd hoped
you would. Let me just serve Jennie and Calvin,
and then we'll have ours, all right?"

"Yes, ma'am, Miss Ipswich," Hutch said.

Evangeline heard him rather collapse into
one kitchen chair at the table, exhaling a heavy,
weary-sounding sigh.

"It sounds as if you've had a long day," she
ventured.

"Yep," he confirmed, "though not as long
as yours, I daresay. I bet you're worn out from
traveling, hmm?"

Evangeline shrugged. "Not so much," she
answered as she took two bowls down from a
cupboard and began ladling stew into them. She
smiled. "And it's so wonderful to be with Jennie
again." She giggled to herself. "I'd forgotten how
amusing she can be." She added a biscuit to each
bowl and said, "I'll be right back," to Hutch as
she headed for the bedroom.

Jennie was sitting up in the bed, Calvin beside her.

"It's hot, you two, so be careful," Evangeline said, handing Calvin his bowl and then Jennie hers. She reached into her apron pocket, retrieving two spoons and two napkins. "I'll bring some water in, if you like."

"Oh, don't go to all that trouble," Calvin assured her. "We've got Jennie's water glass here." He nodded toward the nightstand. "We'll share that for now. You head on in and feed Hutch. He's gotta be near to starving! I don't think he took time to eat at midday today."

"Well, let me know if you need second helpings or anything, all right?" Evangeline asked.

She watched with satisfaction and joy as Jennie placed her face over her steaming bowl of chicken stew and an herb biscuit. "Oh, Evangeline," she sighed. "This smells simply delicious! Thank you so much."

"Let's hope it's as good as it smells then," Evangeline said. "Enjoy. And do let me know if you need anything else."

"Thank you so much, Miss Ipswich," Calvin said with a sincere smile.

"You're welcome," Evangeline said.

She returned to the kitchen, surprised to see Hutch standing at the stove, ladling stew into two bowls on the counter.

"I hope you don't mind," he said, looking

over his shoulder to her. "I just couldn't wait. It smells so good!" He took two biscuits out of the biscuit pan, plopping one on top of the stew in each bowl. "And besides," he said as he strode to the table and placed one bowl on either side of it, "you worked hard making supper. Seems to me you deserve to be served more than I do."

Evangeline smiled and bit her lip with delight as Hutch pulled her chair out for her, scooting it in as she sat.

"Thank you," she said.

Hutch hurried to a kitchen drawer and retrieved two spoons, returning to the table and handing one to Evangeline.

Quickly he clasped his hands together, bowed his head, and said, "Thank you, Lord, for this delicious meal, prepared by two beautiful hands. Amen."

Before Evangeline had even finished her own, "Amen," Hutch had plunged his spoon into the stew and taken his first bite.

"Oh, be careful, Hutch! It's very hot!" Evangeline warned too late.

"It's all right," Hutch said, however, as he puffed a bit of steam from his mouth. "I like my stew hot." He took a bite of his biscuit and moaned, "Mmmm mmmm mmm!" He sighed and then said, "I never thought I'd hear myself say this . . ."

"But you were tired of bacon?" Evangeline finished, smiling at him.

Hutch chuckled and nodded as he took another bite of stew. "Jennie told you, huh?"

"She did," Evangeline admitted.

"Well, me and Calvin only know how to cook two things between us—and one's bacon and eggs," he explained. "We knew bacon and eggs would be best for Jennie and the baby, being that jerky and hardtack were the only other things we each knew how to make."

"I'm sure she's very grateful," Evangeline offered. She shook her head. "Anything sounds better than hardtack."

Hutch continued to smile. "I *can* make oatmeal too," he said. "But Jennie hates oatmeal, so me and Calvin stuck to the bacon and eggs."

Evangeline took a bite of her own stew, and as it traveled down her throat, it warmed her from head to toe. In fact, she hadn't even realized that she'd been a little chilled until the stew began to warm her from the inside out.

"I'm glad you told me that Jennie doesn't like oatmeal, because I do, and I might have made it for her otherwise," Evangeline said.

She watched, flattered and very pleased as she noticed that Hutch was nearly finished with his bowl of stew before she'd even taken her third bite.

As he stood up with his bowl in hand and strode

She began to giggle when she heard Jennie laugh.

"I'm having my seconds on stew and biscuits first," Jennie called.

"She's eating like a horse back there, Evangeline," Calvin chuckled. He placed a biscuit in both his and Jennie's bowls that were once more filled with stew. Then he turned and smiled at Evangeline. "Thank you for coming. Thank you so very much," he said.

Evangeline smiled in return, moved by Calvin's obvious sincerity.

"Thank you for having me, Calvin," she told him.

Calvin nodded and started back toward the bedroom and his wife. He paused a moment, however, looked back over his shoulder, and said, "Hey, Hutch."

"Yep?" Hutch acknowledged, looking to his brother-in-law.

"Jennie told me she didn't have time to show you to the spare room where Evangeline will be staying," Calvin explained. "Do you think you could set her up in there for me before you leave?" Calvin lowered his voice, adding, "Jennie's really worn out tonight."

But Hutch frowned. "Oh," he rather mumbled, a look of confused concern on his face. "Well, I thought Evangeline would just be bunking in with me while she's here. My bed's plenty big enough for two."

Evangeline gasped with astonished chagrin. But as Hutch smiled and winked at her, indicating he was teasing, she blushed—still a little breathless, nevertheless.

Calvin burst into laughter, however. "Seems to me you've forgotten what a tease Hutch is, Evangeline," he chortled.

"What? Is she blushing?" Jennie called. "Is she embarrassed? Are you embarrassed, Evangeline? Oh, I'm missing *everything* by having to stay in bed!"

"Oh, simmer down, Jennie," Evangeline heard Calvin say as he entered the bedroom. "I'm sure you'll have plenty more chances to see Hutch mortify your friend."

Evangeline shook her head with mingled amusement and sudden fatigue. "It seems I'll have to have my wits about me when you're around, Hutch LaMontagne."

"It seems so," Hutch agreed, grinning at her.

Just his expression as he smiled at her—just the realization that there was only a tabletop between herself and the most attractive man she had ever known in all her life—caused a thrill to travel over her. Goose bumps prickled her arms and legs, and Evangeline forced her attention away from Hutch and to the bowl of stew on the table before her.

Hutchner LaMontagne, she thought. It had been several years since Evangeline had finally been able to reconcile herself to never seeing him again. And yet there he was—sitting across the table from her, smiling at her as he enjoyed her chicken stew.

CHAPTER FIVE

The first week of Evangeline's visit with Jennie seemed to fly by. Although Jennie needed a lot of rest (and Evangeline saw to it that she napped every few hours throughout the day), there was a lot to do to keep up the household chores and meals for her dear friend. Washing, dusting, dishes to be cleaned—it all kept Evangeline very busy and quite worn out by the end of the day. She hadn't realized how little housework she'd really needed to do at home. After all, Kizzy kept the house so clean and fresh and looked after Shay. Amoretta and Calliope had their own homes to tend. Somehow Evangeline had slipped into only caring for her own needs or cooking an occasional meal to give Kizzy a rest.

Thus, as Evangeline cared for Jennie and her home, she realized that, when she did return to Meadowlark Lake, she needed to make some serious changes in her life. It was time her father, Kizzy, and Shay (and the new baby) had their own home. Evangeline had decided she would take a room at the boarding house and find a way to earn her own way.

She also made the decision she would not settle into marrying Floyd Longfellow simply because he wanted her and no one else seemed to. No!

Evangeline thought that she really would rather live out her days as a spinster, as opposed to marrying a man she did not love—or wasn't even attracted to in the least!

Admittedly, it was Hutch's presence that had finally woken her up from the despairing daydream of having to settle for marrying Floyd Longfellow. Hutch made Evangeline feel alive— so wildly alive! She'd forgotten how wonderfully alive he had always made her feel—until the moment she'd seen him at the train station, that is. But after a week of seeing Hutch LaMontagne every night for supper, and on any other occasion throughout the day when he chose to stop in at the McKee residence and see how his sister was faring, Evangeline knew that she wanted to feel alive while living—the sort of excitement in living that Hutch inspired in her. Simply the sparkle in Hutch's eyes when he spoke to her about his day at the livery each evening or the way he pampered his three-legged dog with treats from his pockets and frequent scratchings behind the ears—everything about him was more exciting than anything Evangeline had experienced in a very long time.

In truth, she could hardly wait for supper each evening—for Hutch to arrive, beg Jennie to let Jones come into the house and curl up on the entryway rug, remove his hat, and smile at her as he entered the kitchen. Furthermore, almost every evening Hutch and Evangeline spent their meal solely in one another's company, for Calvin preferred to eat his supper with Jennie in the bedroom—and Evangeline was secretly delighted that he did.

And so, after a week in Red Peak, not only had Evangeline made some decisions on how she would change her circumstances once she returned to Meadowlark Lake, but also she'd begun to enjoy the hard work of caring for Jennie and Calvin. She especially enjoyed Jennie's waking hours, when the two of them would sit together in Jennie's bed, laughing over memories, talking of their new lives, and just sharing conversation and friendship.

And she'd learned so much about the life Jennie had led since she'd left Boston—since Evangeline had left Boston. Naturally, Evangeline's favorite stories were of Jennie and Calvin's meeting—of their falling in love and their move to Red Peak. Evangeline had grown to admire and appreciate Calvin McKee all the more with every detail Jennie revealed about him. Calvin was a hard-working, sincere man, and it was obvious he loved Jennie more than his own life. Calvin was very affectionate with Jennie—very patient and always concerned for her well-being.

Once in a while a despairing fear would try to creep into Evangeline's mind—a fear that something might happen to Jennie when it was her time to have the baby. When the thought did try to take hold of her courage and begin to cause her to imagine the pain Calvin would know if something did go wrong, Evangeline would simply whisper a silent prayer and send despairing thoughts scampering back to oblivion. Evangeline would not be able to endure watching Calvin lose Jennie. She wondered if she could even endure it—though she had endured losing her mother and knew that if she could endure that, she could endure . . .

"What're you so lost in thought about this morning?" Hutch asked, stepping through the front door. "Jones," he mumbled, pointing to the entryway rug.

Evangeline smiled as Hutch's three-legged companion curled up on the rug, exhaled a heavy sigh, and closed his eyes.

"Oh, nothing worth mentioning," Evangeline answered. "What brings you by? Just checking in on Jennie?"

"Yeah. There's not much going on over at the livery right now," Hutch explained. "So I thought I'd look in on her. Is she sleeping?"

"Not *now!*" Jennie called from the bedroom. "Not with all the clattering around you make when you come into the house, Hutch."

Evangeline grinned and said, "I think she's awake."

Hutch smiled in return, saying, "Sounds like it."

"Evie, will you bring in those photographs you showed me the other day?" Jennie called. "I would love for Hutch to see them too, if you don't mind."

"Bossy little thing, isn't she?" Hutch whispered, winking conspiratorially at Evangeline.

"I heard that, Hutchner," Jennie giggled from the bedroom.

"I'll get the photographs and be right in, Jen," Evangeline assured her friend—though her gaze and smile lingered on Hutch.

Hutch nodded to Evangeline and headed into Jennie's bedroom.

"How are you faring this morning, sweetie?" she heard him ask his sister.

"Well enough," Jennie answered with a sigh. "Though I'm getting pretty tired of being in bed all the time. It'll be so nice to be up and around again once the baby comes."

Evangeline hurried to the spare room where she'd been staying. Quickly she retrieved the small stack of cherished photographs of her family that she'd brought with her from home. Jennie had reveled in delight in studying them for several hours the day Evangeline had shown them to her. She hoped Hutch would enjoy them too.

When she arrived in Jennie's room, it was to see Jennie happily sitting up in the middle of the bed, with Hutch sitting on the bed next to her on her right.

Patting the empty space on the bed to her left, Jennie said, "Oh, goody! Come sit down, Evie!" She looked to her brother and said, "You're going to love seeing how the Ipswich family has changed since we last saw them, Hutch. And Judge Ipswich's wife looks like some beauty out of a storybook!"

Happily, Evangeline sat down next to Jennie.

"Show them to him just the way you first showed them to me, Evie. You know, in order of when they were taken," Jennie excitedly instructed.

Evangeline giggled, pleased by Jennie's enthusiasm about the photographs. She was sure Hutch was simply humoring his sister—that he probably could not have cared less about seeing photographs of the Ipswich family. Still, it was making Jennie happy to share them, so she would.

"All right," Evangeline began. She took a large, mounted photograph from the bottom of the pile. "This is the family photograph we had taken two years before we left Boston," she explained. She passed the panel card to Jennie. "It's the first photograph we had taken after Mother passed away."

"This is how I remember you all looking, Evie," Jennie said. "I've thought of you this way ever since we parted." She smiled as she handed the panel card to Hutch. "But you're even more beautiful now—all grown up and a proper lady!"

"A proper lady, hmm?" Evangeline laughed. "I think not."

"You Ipswich girls always were the talk of the town, you know," Hutch said as he studied the photograph. "At least, among the boys and young men."

"I've already planned on you for supper tonight, Hutch," Evangeline playfully told him. "No need to butter me up."

Hutch chuckled and continued to study the photograph. Evangeline smiled, pleased that his interest in it was sincere.

"And next?" Jennie prodded impatiently.

"And next . . . well, this one is of Father and Kizzy on their wedding day," Evangeline said, taking a cabinet card from the pile. She gazed at it a moment, admiring how dashingly handsome her father was, at how Kizzy's beauty seemed so ethereal. "The handsome groom and his beautiful bride," she said, handing the mounted photograph to Jennie.

Jennie held the photograph of Lawson Ipswich and his stunning young bride with both hands, smiling and sighing with approval.

"Oh, your father is as handsome as ever, Evie!" she said.

"I remember the day Mama told you that you wouldn't be able to marry Mr. Ipswich when you grew up," Hutch teased as his sister handed him

81

the cabinet card photograph. "I think that about broke your little heart."

Evangeline watched Hutch closely as he studied her father's wedding photograph. She watched his eyebrows arch in admiration.

"My, my, my," he said. "Your father looks to be as intimidating a man as ever he was." He whistled approval and said, "And looks to me like it would take a man the likes of Lawson Ipswich to reel himself in a woman like this."

"Evangeline's stepmother is a gypsy!" Jennie offered.

"So I've been told once before," Hutch said. He looked to Evangeline.

"Now show him little Shay," Jennie prodded.

Drawing the cabinet card photograph of Shay from the pile, Evangeline handed it to Jennie.

"What a little angel," Jennie sighed. "Those eyes! They just capture a body's very soul somehow."

Jennie handed the photograph of Shay to Hutch, and he chuckled. "So this is your little sister then, hmmm? The one that drags her cat around on a leash?"

Evangeline giggled. "Oh, there's no dragging Molly anywhere she doesn't want to go. Shay has leash-trained her."

"Well, she's a pretty little thing, isn't she?" Hutch commented. "I'm sure she'll be breaking a lot of boys' hearts along the way." His smile

82

broadened. "And am I correct in assuming that this is the infamous leash-trained cat she's holding?"

Evangeline laughed, just as she did most times when she looked at the photograph of Shay, holding Molly around the waist while the cat drooped lackadaisically to one side.

"Yep! That's Molly, the feline with the patience of Job," Evangeline confirmed.

"Now Amoretta and Brake," Jennie whispered.

Handing another cabinet card to Jennie, Evangeline explained to Hutch, "And this is the one that should confirm to you that we really are all grown up. This is Amoretta and her husband, Brake, on their wedding day."

Jennie handed the photograph to Hutch, and Evangeline grinned when his eyebrows arched in astonishment.

"This is little Amoretta?" he asked. He shook his head and smiled. "It's hard to believe. Time travels fast, doesn't it?"

"It definitely does," Jennie agreed.

"Daddy and Amoretta were married the same day, but I didn't bring the large photograph of the whole group," Evangeline said.

"Oh, I wish you would've," Jennie sighed. "I would love to have seen everyone all together."

"I'll bring it next time," Evangeline told her friend.

Jennie smiled and nodded. "Now the Tom Thumb wedding, Evie," Jennie instructed.

Evangeline giggled, pleased that Jennie was enjoying herself so much.

"Now this," Evangeline began, "is a photograph of the entire cast of the Tom Thumb wedding Calliope orchestrated for Meadowlark Lake."

"You helped too," Jennie reminded.

"Yes, but it was all Calliope's idea." Evangeline handed the large panel card directly to Hutch.

"Aw, yes!" he exclaimed. "I fell victim to having to play the groom in one of these damn things when I was about eight."

"Don't swear in front of Evie, Hutch," Jennie scolded in a whisper.

But Evangeline laughed, remembering how unwilling the groom in the Meadowlark Lake Tom Thumb wedding had been at first.

"Warren Ackerman, our groom, probably would've sworn if he thought he could've gotten away with it," Evangeline admitted.

"But your pretty little sister was the bride," Hutch noted. "And I'm assuming that made everything all right with your groom in the end?"

Evangeline laughed. "Yes. Shay won him over, and Warren made it through admirably."

"And Calliope got married that very day!" Jennie exclaimed. "Right after the Tom Thumb wedding." Overwrought with excitement, Jennie snatched the last cabinet card photograph from

Evangeline's lap, handing it to Hutch. "Can you believe this is little Calliope?"

Hutch again shook his head. "It's kind of hard to take in, all these little girls I once knew, grown up and married."

All but one, Evangeline thought to herself.

She watched as Hutch carefully shuffled the photographs, settling once more on the one of Evangeline's father and Kizzy.

"So your daddy's wife is really a gypsy?" he asked.

Evangeline exchanged amused glances with Jennie.

"Yes," she answered. "Well, she's got gypsy ancestry and knows their ways," she explained. "And she is different a bit from what we're all used to—not quite eccentric exactly, just . . . herself."

"How so?" Hutch asked.

Evangeline shrugged. "Well, she doesn't ever wear her hair up the way that is considered proper." She smiled, adding, "But Daddy prefers it down."

"I bet he does," Hutch chuckled.

"And Evangeline says she rarely wears shoes or slippers when she's in the house," Jennie continued.

"And every dress, skirt, blouse, and scarf she wears seems so light and flowing—colorful too," Evangeline added. She shrugged. "It's rather hard to explain. One has to meet Kizzy to understand her unique beauty of face and spirit."

"And you say she's going to have a baby?" he asked.

Again Evangeline smiled. "Yes, she is. Close to Thanksgiving."

Hutch's laughter drew her mind from its reveries.

"What's so amusing?" Jennie asked her brother.

Evangeline couldn't help but smile at Hutch, for the very brightness of his handsome smile was enough to make the sun envious.

"I just can't imagine those little Ipswich girls grown up and getting married," he explained. He exhaled a sigh, shook his head once more, and added, "Makes me feel near to *ancient*." He leaned over and kissed Jennie on the cheek. "But I guess my own little sister is married and having a baby, so it stands to reason everyone else has grown up too."

Hutch offered the stack of photographs to Evangeline. Yet as she reached out to accept them, Jennie asked, "Oh, can't I look at them just a bit longer, Evie? I'm just enchanted by seeing everyone again."

Evangeline smiled. "Of course, Jen," she said.

Hutch gently deposited the photographs on Jennie's lap, kissed her forehead, and stood up from the bed.

"I better be getting back to the livery," he

said. He snapped his fingers as if just having remembered something. "Oh, Evangeline," he began, taking an envelope from his back pocket, "Calvin said there was a letter for you at the postal office when he stopped by this morning. I told him I'd hand it off to you."

"Thank you," Evangeline said, accepting the envelope he offered. Evangeline smiled. "It's Daddy's hand on the addressing. News from home!"

"Oh, good!" Jennie said. "Why don't you read it to me later . . . after I've rested a bit."

Evangeline frowned as she looked at Jennie then. Her friend looked paler than she had a moment before—and suddenly very fatigued.

"Are you feeling all right, Jennie?" Hutch asked, having obviously noticed the quick change in his sister's demeanor and appearance as well.

"Just tired," Jennie said. She picked up the photographs that had been lying on her lap, offering them to Evangeline with trembling hands. "I just need a little rest, that's all."

"Of course," Evangeline said—though anxiety began to rise in her.

"You have a good day, Hutch," Jennie mumbled as she closed her eyes. "I'll see you for supper."

"All right, sweetheart," Hutch said, also frowning. "You rest now."

Hutch looked to Evangeline, nodding toward

the bedroom door in gesturing she should follow him out of the room.

Once they were both in the kitchen, he asked in a whisper, "I didn't like the looks of that, did you?"

Evangeline shook her head. "No, indeed not!"

"Do you think I should fetch Calvin home?" he asked.

Evangeline nodded, swallowing the lump of uneasiness that was forming in her throat. "Hutch . . . I think you should fetch Doctor Swayze too. Just to be safe."

"I think you're right," Hutch mumbled as he headed for the door.

Jones instantly hopped up on all three legs to greet his master. But Hutch said, "You stay put, Jones. I'll be right back."

Hutch grabbed his hat from the hat rack and, with a final nod of reassurance to Evangeline, left the house.

CHAPTER SIX

"Mrs. McKee has a slight fever," Doctor Swayze explained to Calvin. Evangeline stood nearby, listening with deep concern. Hutch was there as well, frowning. He kept rubbing the whiskers of his chin and jaw, and Evangeline knew he was worried too. Why wouldn't he be? Evangeline and Hutch had been sitting on Jennie's bed with her looking at photographs and enjoying light, merry conversation one moment, and Jennie had gone pale and weak the next!

"Is she all right?" Calvin asked.

Evangeline stared at the doctor, studying his countenance as he spoke.

"So far, yes," the doctor answered. "Let's hope she's just a bit under the weather." He looked to Evangeline, however, adding, "But I also checked her where the coming of the baby is concerned, and I believe the baby will come early, Miss Ipswich. You need to be watchful for me—especially if you see any fluid escape her or if she begins having her pains. All right?"

Evangeline nodded. "Of course," she assured him.

"What else can we do, Doc?" Hutch asked.

Evangeline reached out and took Calvin's hand, squeezing it with a gesture of offering reassurance. Calvin had suddenly gone nearly as pale as his wife had, and Evangeline knew the fear he was experiencing—for she'd experienced a similar fear in her own past, just before her mother and baby brother had passed away from complications of childbirth.

"Just keep a watchful eye on her and notify me if anything changes," Doctor Swayze answered. "At this point, I'd have someone sit with her around the clock, even when she's resting."

"I'll stay in her room when she's alone, at all times," Evangeline assured the men with a nod to each in turn.

"I'll be fine," Jennie called from the bedroom. "You all worry too much. I won't be wearing out Evangeline with playing nursemaid to me!"

Everyone smiled, and Hutch said, "Sounds like she's feeling a little better anyway."

Evangeline did feel somewhat relieved at the sound of Jennie's reassuring voice.

"Keep a watchful eye on her, all of you," Doctor Swayze whispered. "And don't hesitate to call for me if you have any questions or concerns."

"Thanks, Doc," Calvin said, shaking Doctor Swayze's hand gratefully.

Calvin opened the door to allow Doctor Swayze to leave. There was a young woman standing on the front porch, poised as if she'd just begun to knock on the door.

"Oh my! Hello there, Doctor Swayze," the

very pretty young woman greeted. A frown of concern puckered her lovely brow as she asked, "Is everything all right? I just came by to peek in on Mrs. McKee, to see if she was faring well, so I'm a little befuddled to see you here, Doctor."

"Mrs. McKee is doing just fine, Miss Griffiths," Doctor Swayze said.

The lovely young woman with brown hair and green eyes put a dainty, graceful hand to her bosom and said, "Oh, thank heaven!" Looking past Doctor Swayze then—and even Calvin—the young woman gazed directly at Hutch and asked, "Is there anything I can do to help your sister, Mr. LaMontagne?"

Evangeline noted the manner in which Hutch's posture stiffened a bit. "Nope. We have things well in hand, Heather. But thank you all the same," he kindly, but almost tersely, answered.

"Are you sure?" the woman named Heather asked. She looked to Evangeline, arching one eyebrow as if she'd only just met an archenemy.

"We're sure," Calvin answered. "In fact, my Jennie's dear friend has traveled up to stay with her until the baby comes, so we're just fine."

"Hmm," Heather hummed. She looked to Hutch again, smiling as if she'd only just opened a door to find a horde of gold piled up in front of her. "Well, you'll let me know if there's anything I can do, won't you, Hutchner?"

"Yes, ma'am," Hutch said with a nod.

"You have a good day, Heather," Calvin said, closing the door then.

Hutch and Calvin both exhaled heavy sighs of what appeared to be relief and exchanged understanding glances.

"Calvin! Hutch!" Jennie called in a loud whisper from the bedroom. "Evie, bring those two into me right now!" she added.

Evangeline giggled, smiled at Calvin, and said, "I think she is feeling better, Calvin."

Calvin chuckled and hurried into the bedroom.

"You too, Hutch," Jennie called.

When Evangeline entered the bedroom just before Hutch, she audibly sighed with relief. Jennie did indeed look much better. In fact, the pink had returned to her cheeks, and her eyes were sparkling with mischief.

"Was that Heather Griffiths I heard at the door?" Jennie asked in a still lowered voice.

"Indeed it was," Hutch almost moaned.

Somewhat absentmindedly, Evangeline went to the window of Jennie and Calvin's bedroom, gazing through the sheer curtains and watching Heather Griffiths rather wiggle her way across the street.

"She's getting mighty brazen, Hutch," Jennie laughed. "What're you gonna do when she corners you alone one day, hmmm?"

"Are you courting her, Hutch?" Evangeline asked before she could stop herself. The hot

92

anxiety of jealousy was smoldering in her bosom—even though she had no right to feel it.

But when Calvin, Hutch, and Jennie all three burst into laughter, Evangeline turned to see Hutch shaking his head emphatically as he repeated, "No! No, no, no, never!"

"Remember how you explained to me about Amoretta's husband, Brake, Evie?" Jennie asked. "How all the girls in town were doe-eyes and puppy slobbers over him?"

"Yes," Evangeline assured her.

"Well, it isn't any different here in Red Peak where the handsome Hutchner LaMontagne is concerned," Jennie explained. "And no woman in town is more improperly forward in her obvious desire to win Hutch for herself than Miss Heather Griffiths."

"That's enough," Hutch grumbled. "I don't want to talk about that . . . not at all."

Evangeline looked to Hutch and then back to Jennie. Jennie still wore a smile of amusement stretching from ear to ear, at her brother's expense.

"So am I to understand you're not courting her?" Evangeline asked Hutch.

"Oh, hell no!" Hutch growled, frowning.

"I told you not to swear in front of Evangeline, Hutch," Jennie playfully scolded.

Calvin chuckled, adding, "Heather Griffiths is after Hutch as serious as a hound dog chasing a

93

rabbit! She pretty much makes his life miserable at least four days a week. Isn't that right, Hutch?"

It was obvious Hutch was uncomfortable—uncomfortable with Heather Griffiths's pursuit of him, as well as being the topic of conversation in the room. Evangeline tried not to smile—tried not to be amused by his discomfort—but she couldn't help it, and she smiled at him when he glared at her.

"Hey," Calvin exclaimed, snapping his fingers, "I've got it!" He turned to Evangeline and said, "Why don't you just take Hutchner here as your lover, Evangeline? Then Jennie and I can spread some mild gossip about it, and Heather Griffiths will run for the hills where Hutch is concerned."

"What?" Evangeline exclaimed in an astonished whisper.

"Yes, that's a wonderful idea, Calvin!" Jennie agreed with enthusiasm. "That would work just fine!"

"I do hope you all are teasing!" Evangeline scolded, blushing to the tips of her toes.

"Why?" Hutch asked her. "Don't you think I'd make a good lover?"

Evangeline shook her head and said, "Now you all are just being plain ridiculous with your teasing!" Almost roughly Evangeline began to straighten the curtains in Jennie's bedroom. "Why, I've never heard of such a thing! Starting

94

terrible gossip and ruining my reputation just to keep Hutchner from being bothered by an admirer."

She gasped, however, when Hutch took hold of her shoulders and turned her to face him. "I'd be a good lover for you, Evie," he said. His voice was low and shamelessly seductive. "And I'll be gentle and—"

"Hutch!" Evangeline exclaimed—though she found she was simultaneously chagrined and delighted. "Stop that this minute!"

Hutch smiled triumphantly and released Evangeline.

"Now, don't think I'm naive to the way married people tease others. I've got married sisters of my own." She looked to Calvin, grinned, and winked. "And a couple of very mischievous brothers-in-law to boot. Furthermore, I know you are all just having your jollies at my expense . . . but really! To tease about such a thing!"

Hutch's handsome brow furrowed a little. "I bet Heather Griffiths would be glad to have me for a lover. What makes you think I wouldn't be good enough for *you?*"

Jennie and Calvin burst into laughter, and when Hutch smiled and winked at her, Evangeline realized the entire scene had been played out simply to make Jennie feel better. Therefore, she thought she'd forgive Hutch his taunting.

"Oh, I'm sure you would be, Mr. LaMontagne,"

Evangeline told him then. "But I've got supper to tend to."

Evangeline hurried to the bed, kissed Jennie on one cheek, and said, "I'm so glad you're feeling better, Jen. I'll make sure supper is something that won't be too much for your stomach, all right?" She stood then, glancing from Calvin to Hutch and back. "Meanwhile, you two little devils go on about your mischief. Just keep an eye on our Jennie while you do."

Evangeline hurried to the kitchen, anxious to escape any more teasing, for her stomach was in a tangle of mixed emotions. The thought of Hutch—of having an intimate relationship with him—had not only caused her to blush and feel flustered but also caused her heart to soar! It was obvious he was as thoroughly woven into her dreams and desires as ever he had been when they were in Boston—more so! And that realization was frightening.

Evangeline knew she would be leaving in a few weeks. After Jennie had the baby and had recovered well enough, Evangeline would return to Meadowlark Lake—to her life of being the spinster older Ipswich sister, fodder for Floyd Longfellow's attentions. It wasn't as if Hutch were going to suddenly find himself in love with her the way Calvin had Jennie. It wasn't as if he were going to suddenly drop to one knee and ask her to marry him. No. He would go about his life in Red Peak, and she would return to hers in Meadowlark Lake.

And so Evangeline went about preparing supper for Jennie and the men. She tried to think only of Jennie—of her need for something soothing and not too hard on her stomach. Soup was always a good choice for anyone who wasn't feeling quite up to snuff. And so Evangeline decided a nice, hearty vegetable soup of potatoes, carrots, dried basil, and any other vegetables on hand would do.

"Sorry about that all that in there," Hutch said from behind her suddenly. "But it did cheer Jennie up, you know."

"Oh, I know," Evangeline said, trying to make her voice sound as normal and unaffected as possible.

She heard a chair slide away from the table—heard Hutch let out a heavy sigh as he sat down.

"She worries me so much," he confessed. "When the doc told Calvin Jennie would have to stay in bed until the baby came, I'll be honest with you, Evie—it put me in mind of your mother. And that frightens me."

At once Evangeline's embarrassment evaporated into empathy. She turned and offered a reassuring smile to Hutch. "I know. I thought of the same thing when her letter arrived telling me what Doctor Swayze's orders were," she

97

confessed. "She mentioned to me that she also thought of my mother." She looked away a moment. "It actually took quite a bit of courage for me to come here to be with her, because I was afraid that something might happen to Jennie or the baby . . . or both." She looked back to him, again offering a comforting smile. "And today's events didn't do anything to strengthen my backbone."

Hutch shook his head and agreed, "Mine either." His expression brightened, however, and he added, "She seems pretty perked up now though, doesn't she?"

"She does. Maybe she was just overly tired," Evangeline agreed. "We'll get some warm soup in her and make sure she goes to sleep early. Rest is the best thing for her."

"I sure am glad you're here, Evangeline," Hutch sighed, raking a hand through his hair. "Calvin and I . . . well, we may have appeared like we were handling everything all right, but the truth is, both of us were about one more day away from having to be put in the insanity asylum, you know?"

"You both did wonders, and you are *still* doing wonders," Evangeline assured him. "I'm just happy I can help."

"I am still offended, however, though," Hutch said then.

"Offended about what?" Evangeline asked as

she pumped water into the sink to rinse some carrots for the soup.

"That you don't want to take me for your lover," Hutch answered.

He chuckled, and Evangeline couldn't help but giggle as well. Turning around, she playfully flung a carrot at him, saying, "You stop talking about such things, Hutch!"

The carrot hit Hutch in the chest, and he caught it as it began to tumble to the floor. Drying the wet vegetable off on his shirt, he bit the end off and started chewing. "Mmm!" he sighed. "I love a good carrot." He continued eating the carrot for a few moments, and Evangeline returned to her task.

Nevertheless, when Hutch had finished the carrot, he said, "But I don't understand it. Jennie once told me that you were sweet on me when you were a girl. How come the idea of taking me as your lover horrifies you so much now?"

Evangeline's cheeks turned as red as red roses. Whirling around to face Hutch, she shrieked in a whisper, "She told you? Jennie told you that I . . . that I used to . . . that I . . ."

"Oh, it was a year or so back," Hutch began to explain, "before you two took to exchanging letters and such. I'm guessing she thought the two of you would never see one another again." He shrugged. "It was right after her and Calvin moved out here. We were talking about Boston and the things we missed, and Jennie said how much she missed you. I told her I always thought you were the prettiest little thing in the city, and she told me that you had eyes for me once." He exhaled a heavy sigh, leaned back in the chair, and added, "I guess I didn't grow up pretty enough for your liking, hmm?"

"I already told you I think you're handsome," Evangeline confessed, blushing a deeper shade of scarlet and turning back to her vegetables. "I told you when you met me at the train station and we were on our way here."

Hutch grinned. "No, you didn't. You told me I was taller than you remembered, not that I was handsome."

Evangeline had to be careful not to cut herself with the paring knife she was using to coin up the carrots. Her hands were trembling so from the conversation Hutch was driving.

"Fine then," she said. "You're very handsome."

"But not handsome enough to be your lover?" he baited.

Shaking her head and continuing to coin carrots, Evangeline said, "Well, your teasing manner has certainly gotten worse over the years." She paused, mumbling, "And I can't believe Jennie told you that I was sweet on you when I was a girl."

"Oh, don't be angry with her," he chuckled. "It's all in fun."

"I'm not angry with her," Evangeline admitted.

She smiled. "I could never be angry with Jennie."

"I still don't see why you won't help me out where that Heather Griffiths is concerned though," Hutch continued to tease. "She's like a burr under my saddle."

Evangeline exhaled a heavy sigh, choosing to ignore Hutch's baiting this time.

There was silence between them for a time, and then Hutch said, "After supper, let's take a deck of cards in and play rummy with Jennie on her bed, all right? I mean, if you won't agree to take me as your lover, the least you can do is play cards with me."

"All right," Evangeline giggled.

Hutch smiled, amused by how easy it was to ruffle Evangeline Ipswich's feathers. He watched her as she continued to cut up vegetables for the soup she was preparing for supper. Land sakes, she was a good cook! Hutch truly could not remember eating food as delicious as the food and meals Evangeline had been preparing since she'd arrived.

And the food she prepared wasn't the only thing delicious about her. Though he'd never forgotten the Ipswich family—especially the eldest and prettiest of the daughters —he'd been nearly knocked off his feet by the ethereal beauty he'd met at the train station. The moment Evangeline had turned and looked up at him, Hutch had been

101

smitten—mesmerized—bewitched. And it wasn't just because Evangeline Ipswich was the most beautiful woman he'd ever seen either—though she certainly was. It was something about her smile, the sparkle to her emerald eyes when she looked at him, something about her very soul that drew him in—as if he'd been mucking around in the mud all his life, and then suddenly . . . the mud was gone and only the beautiful quench of a fresh summer stream remained.

The truth was, if it hadn't been for the fact that Evangeline was in Red Peak to spend time with Jennie—well then, Hutchner would make a grab for her heart. But with Jennie so tired and feeling so poorly—with Calvin and Jennie both needing Evangeline's care—it wouldn't be right to let himself act so selfishly.

Nonetheless, once the baby had arrived safely, Jennie had recovered, and all was well, Hutch was determined to try to win Evangeline Ipswich for himself. And he figured there wasn't any harm in laying a little groundwork by teasing her here and there, having some good conversations over suppers and things.

He watched as she tucked a stray strand of raven hair behind her ear and thought how much he would enjoy it if he truly were her lover.

"You play rummy better than any old granny I ever knew!" Calvin exclaimed to his wife.

Jennie laughed. "And I don't cheat," she assured him. Glaring at her brother, she added, "Not like *some* people in the room used to."

"Hey, I don't cheat!" Hutch defended himself.

He was sitting on a chair next to Jennie's bed. Bending over and studying his cards a moment, he reached out, laying three aces on the bed. "I just win," he playfully gloated.

"Oh, come on, Hutchner!" Calvin moaned. "Give another fellow a chance, will you?"

Evangeline giggled from her position at the foot of Jennie's bed. "The game's not over yet, Calvin. Don't lose heart," she encouraged.

"But he's already won three hands," Calvin reminded. "And Jennie won the two before that."

"Evangeline let me win those two," Jennie said, winking at Evangeline.

"I did not," Evangeline fibbed.

"Well, I think it's adorable that Evie let Jennie win," Hutch said, drawing a card. "I never met anybody in all my life who cheated for other people to win a game."

Evangeline sighed with a moment of pure contentment. It was a lovely evening—a lovely moment. The fire in the bedroom's small hearth had died down to just embers now—beautiful, glowing embers that kept the room just the right kind of warm. Friends were gathered around enjoying an entertaining game of cards,

103

and everyone's stomachs were warm and full of soothing, nourishing soup.

Jennie, specifically, had looked much better after having eaten her first bowl of soup. Evangeline was so glad that the soup seemed to revive her friend, for it had been a worrisome day. But now Jennie seemed full of vim and vigor and was laughing wholeheartedly at the playful comments Hutch and Calvin were ever exchanging.

However, as wonderful moments always seem to do, this one came to an abrupt end all at once.

Jennie gasped and looked up to Evangeline.

"Evie?" she said. "Something's wrong, I think."

"What do you mean?" Evangeline asked, tossing her cards aside and leaning forward to place a hand to Jennie's forehead.

"Well, I'm embarrassed to say," Jennie began, blushing, "but I think I wet the bed."

"Really?" Calvin said, fairly leaping up from his place next to his wife.

Quickly Evangeline climbed off the bed, went to Jennie, and lifted her covers.

"I think maybe it's your waters, Jennie," Evangeline said, attempting to remain calm— especially in appearance.

"My waters?" Jennie exclaimed as a look of panic suddenly owned her expression. "But it's too early! The baby isn't due for at least two more weeks!"

Evangeline forced a smile. "Lots of babies come early or late, Jennie. Don't worry." She looked up to Calvin, though she continued to speak to Jennie. "Calvin will just run on over and fetch Doctor Swayze, and he can have a look at things. Isn't that right, Calvin?"

Calvin was as pale as a sheet, eyes wide with worry and fear.

"Y-yes . . . yes, that's right," he stammered. Forcing a smile of encouragement to Jennie, he stroked her hair and said, "I'll just run on over to fetch Doc Swayze, all right?"

Jennie nodded, though Evangeline noticed the tears welling in her eyes. "All right," she managed.

"I swear, Jennie," Hutch said, stroking his sister's cheek with the back of his hand. "The things you'll do to keep me from winning at rummy."

Jennie laughed a little, smiling at her brother with appreciation.

Jennie's smile faded almost instantly, however, and she said, "Evangeline . . . I don't feel good! And there's . . . there's some pain starting."

Again Evangeline spoke in the calmest voice she could muster, forced a soothing smile, and said, "Well, good! That means that maybe the baby really is on its way! He's tired of waiting to meet his mama and daddy." Still forcing a smile, she nodded to Calvin, reiterating, "You best fetch

Doctor Swayze, Calvin. You'll want to be back so that when the baby comes you can be the first after Jennie to hold it."

Calvin nodded and without another word headed out of the room.

Evangeline then looked to Hutch and asked, "Would you run to the kitchen and fetch a bowl of cool water and a cloth for Jennie's forehead, Hutch. Please?"

Hutch did not look as entirely undone as did Calvin, but Evangeline read the worry in his eyes all the same.

"You bet," he said with a nod. Looking back to Jennie, Hutch also offered an encouraging smile. "I'll be right back, Jen. You just try to relax, all right?"

Jennie nodded, saying, "I will." But once Hutch had left the room, her hand struck Evangeline's with the force of a rattler striking as she took hold of Evangeline's hand. "I'm in a great deal of pain, Evie," she whispered.

"Having a baby is a painful experience, Jennie. You know that, don't you?" Evangeline asked.

"I do," Jennie nodded. "But this pain . . . I'm not sure it's what it should be. It doesn't seem to be subsiding at all. And my back hurts so much that I'm sure I'm going to throw up."

"Well, I'll get a bowl for you, just in case," Evangeline said. "But don't worry, Jennie. Calvin will bring Doctor Swayze, and soon enough your baby will be here, and we can all cuddle and hold it, kiss it, and rock it, and—"

Jennie cried out in agony, startling Evangeline and bringing tears to her own eyes. Thoughts of her own mother—the sounds of her crying out when she'd been having Evangeline's baby brother, Gilbert—pounded through her mind mercilessly, driving remembered and renewed heartache through her body. Her mother and baby brother had died not long after Gilbert was born, and Evangeline's secret fears that the same might happen to her treasured friend Jennie and her baby caused her hands to begin to tremble.

Still, she knew she had to be strong—for Jennie—for the baby. And she said, "Breathe, Jen. Just take long, easy breaths. Doctor Swayze will be here any moment."

Jennie panted a bit, inhaled a deep breath, and then exhaled a heavy sigh. "It's passing now, I think. I think it's passing."

"Oh, good!" Evangeline said. "Good. Now just try to relax."

Evangeline knew that the pain was doing just what Jennie felt it was doing; it was passing. But she further knew that the pain would return—perhaps stronger the next time—and she didn't know what to do to prepare Jennie for it.

Hutch arrived with the bowl of water and the cloth.

"Just wet the cloth and wring it out for me

107

please, will you, Hutch?" Evangeline asked. She was still holding Jennie's hands and trying to keep her calm.

"Of course," Hutch mumbled. He did as Evangeline had instructed and then handed the cool, moist cloth to her.

"There you go," Evangeline soothed as she placed the cloth to Jennie's face a moment. "There. Doesn't that feel good?"

"It's coming on again, Evie!" Jennie cried out, however. "I can feel it coming on!"

"It's all right, Jennie," Evangeline said. "It's the natural way of things, so try to remain as calm as you can. The pain will come, and then it will go again, all right?"

Jennie nodded, and Evangeline could see that she had gritted her teeth—determined to be more courageous through this next pain.

Goose bumps suddenly erupted over Evangeline's shoulders and arms as she felt Hutch's warm, callused hand slip beneath her hair and rest at the back of her neck. Looking up at him, she could see the deep concern on his face. He was worried about his sister.

"Thank you for coming here," he said quietly. He grinned a little, adding, "Can you imagine Calvin and me trying to do this on our own?"

Jennie's sudden burst of laughter surprised Evangeline. "What a . . . what a nightmare that would've been," she puffed. "I can just see the both of them passed out cold on the floor." She laughed again, adding, "Did you see Calvin leap off the bed when I said I thought I'd wet it?"

A nervous giggle erupted from Evangeline then—a strange sound to accompany her admiration of her friend. Even in the throes of excruciating pain, Jennie was still able to find mirth.

As Jennie's laughter turned to tears born of more pain, Hutch moaned with sympathy for his sister.

Looking up to him, Evangeline said, "Dig your heels in, Hutch. It may be a long night."

CHAPTER SEVEN

It has been nearly three hours since Calvin had returned to the house with Doctor Swayze and his wife. And Doctor Swayze was concerned. He felt that Jennie's body should be further along in being ready to deliver the baby. Yet he had assured Hutch and Evangeline that they should remain calm and that all would be well.

Evangeline still sat on the floor just outside Jennie's bedroom. Jones's head was in her lap, and though she gently stroked the velvet of one of his ears with reassurance, even Hutch's dog knew that Jennie was enduring overwhelming pain on the other side of the door.

Hutch had taken to pacing back and forth up and down the entryway, to and fro. Every few minutes, Jennie would cry out, moan, or strain aloud, and Hutch's brows would furrow as he looked to Evangeline for reassurance. Each time he did, Evangeline would nod at him—a silent reminder that such sounds of agony and trauma were to be expected.

Yet even Evangeline was not so certain all was well in the room where Jennie struggled to deliver her baby. Even with the help of Doctor Swayze and his wife—even with the fact that Calvin had demanded to be present, to hold

111

Jennie's hand and attempt to offer her comfort—Evangeline thought Jennie's cries sounded too desperate.

All at once the door to the bedroom burst open, and a frantic, disheveled Calvin appeared.

"Hutch," he breathed. "Fetch the Reverend Lloyd. Hurry!"

Evangeline's eyes filled with tears as she saw Hutch's jaw clench, even as he nodded his assurance to Calvin that he would do what he'd asked. Without even pausing to retrieve his coat and hat, Hutch fairly bolted out the front door.

"Calvin?" Evangeline breathed.

Calvin took a deep breath and said, "She wants to talk to you, Evangeline."

Nodding, Evangeline kindly pushed Jones from her lap and stood up. The dog whimpered, and she looked down at him, forcing a smile and saying, "Everything will be fine, Jones. Don't worry."

Of course, Evangeline knew that everything would obviously not be fine. Calvin had asked Hutch to fetch the local clergyman, and now Jennie had asked to talk to Evangeline. Her heart told her all was not well.

Slowly, she entered Jennie's room, her heart filled with dread. Jennie was lying on her left side in the bed, pale and weak looking.

"Evangeline!" she whispered—and Evangeline did not miss the extreme anxiety in her voice.

"Please come here . . . quickly!" Jennie breathed.

Evangeline looked to Doctor Swayze, who nodded. "It's going to be a difficult birth," he said. "Long and arduous, I'm afraid."

Doctor Swayze was a good-looking, middle-aged man with brown hair and round-framed spectacles. Yet Evangeline thought he looked ten years older in that moment than he had when he'd first arrived several hours previous.

Mrs. Swayze was sitting on the foot of the bed, folding clean washcloths. She did not look up to greet Evangeline, and Evangeline's heart sank to the very pit of her stomach.

"Evie, hurry!" Jennie begged.

Racing to her bedside, Evangeline knelt next to her friend. Forcing a comforting smile and tenderly brushing the perspiration-saturated hair from her forehead, she said, "Jennie, you're doing a wonderful job. Having a baby is no easy thing."

"The doctor thinks the baby is very big," Jennie breathed. "Or . . . or that something is wrong," Jennie told her. "And I want to beg a favor of you . . . please."

"Anything, darling. You know that," Evangeline whispered, trying hard not to cry. She knew exactly what Jennie was going to ask—that she stay in Red Peak and care for her baby if Jennie herself should lose her life in bringing the baby into the world. Tears welled in her eyes, and

Evangeline fought to keep them from spilling. But she couldn't, and they escaped into warm, salty rivulets over her cheeks.

"I want you to marry Hutchner," Jennie whispered. "I can't think of him being alone here . . . alone in the world if I go."

"Jennie!" Evangeline quietly exclaimed. "Doctor Swayze says you'll be—"

"Please, Evie!" Jennie begged as more tears flooded her cheeks. "A woman knows things . . . feels things . . . senses things that a doctor can't. And I need to know that Hutch won't be alone. And more than that . . . that he'll have you to care for him." Jennie's whisper dropped to a mere breath as she added, "That he'll have you to love him, Evie."

Evangeline was awestruck! She wondered if Jennie were in her right mind. She looked up to Calvin—Calvin standing strong but frightened for his wife's well-being. He nodded, his silent gesture that he wanted Evangeline to agree to Jennie's request.

For a moment, Evangeline thought, *Where's the harm in promising it?* If her friend were indeed preparing to make her way to heaven, then who was Evangeline to refuse her last request? It wasn't as if Hutch would have to go through with marrying her, after all. And did he even know what Jennie was asking of Evangeline?

At that very moment, Hutch strode into the

bedroom with a clergyman in his wake. He too knelt beside Jennie, kissed her hand, and said, "I've brought Reverend Lloyd, Jen. But you're gonna be fine. Do you hear me?"

Jennie weakly caressed her brother's whiskery cheek and smiled at him. "Hutch," she began, again in a whisper. "Will you do something for me, Hutch?"

"Anything, Jen. You know that," Hutch answered.

Evangeline watched as moisture filled Hutch's eyes—as emotion caused his hands to begin trembling where he held his sister's.

"I want you to marry Evangeline, Hutch," Jennie began. "Promise me you'll marry her. I don't want you to be without her . . . and I don't want her to be without you. Promise me you'll marry her."

Evangeline held her breath—waited for Hutch's response—wondered if he would be as astonished as she had been at Jennie's request.

"All right, I promise," he said, however. Evangeline felt her mouth gape open with astonishment.

But Jennie's requests were not finished. "Marry her now, Hutch—right here, so I'll know you'll both be cared for . . . so I'll know you'll be together. It's why I had you fetch Reverend Lloyd."

Evangeline couldn't breathe for a moment! Was

115

she dreaming? Was Jennie actually demanding that her brother marry Evangeline?

"All right," Hutch said without pause.

Evangeline closed her eyes a moment—concentrated on simply trying to draw breath.

But she was startled from her weakness of mind and body when Jennie cried out in sudden returning agony!

"Please, Evie! Please!" Jennie cried through her pain. "I need to know that it's done! I need to have that peace!"

"Of course, of course!" Evangeline assured her, brushing tears from her own cheeks.

Hutch took Evangeline's chin in one of his strong hands, forcing her to look at him. "You'll do this thing with me, won't you?" It was a demand, not a request. "For Jennie."

"O-of course," Evangeline answered in a whisper.

Hutch turned to Reverend Lloyd—a tall, spindly man, dressed all in black and with graying hair that stood up on his head as if it were wire driven into his scalp.

"Marry us, Reverend Lloyd," Hutch rather ordered. Realizing then the tone of his demand, he halfheartedly added, "If you please, sir."

"Hurry! Hurry, Reverend Lloyd!" Jennie begged through her own tears. "Marry them before I . . . before I'm gone."

Evangeline wiped her tears on her sleeve. It

couldn't be happening. Jennie couldn't be dying! Not after everything—not after they'd only just become so close once more!

"P-please join hands," Reverend Lloyd instructed, nodding first to Hutch and then to Evangeline.

Evangeline trembled at Hutch's touch. Even for the tragedy that was upon them all, his mere touch caused her pleasure.

"Here now, Jennie," Doctor Swayze said, suddenly speaking. "Brace your leg over my shoulder here . . . but do not push until I tell you it's all right to, do you understand?"

"Do you, Hutchner LaMontagne—" Reverend Lloyd began.

"I do," Hutch growled. He was nearly glaring at Evangeline as he knelt next to her. Yet she knew his glaring was for the fear of losing his sister, not in disgust with Evangeline.

"Very well. Uh . . ." Reverend Lloyd stammered. "Do you, Evangeline . . . I'm sorry, I've forgotten your last—"

"Ipswich," Hutch grumbled with impatience. "Evangeline Ipswich."

"Oh yes," Reverend Lloyd choked. "Do you, Evangeline Ipswich, take Hutchner LaMontagne as your lawfully wedded husband? To have and to—"

"Yes! Yes!" Evangeline cried.

"Well then . . . I, by the powers invested in me,

now pronounce you man and wife," the reverend abruptly finished. Closing the Bible he'd been holding when he walked into the room, he added, "You m-may kiss the bride."

"Kiss the bride?" Evangeline cried as more tears streamed over her face. "Are you mad?" she cried, looking at the reverend in astonishment.

Evangeline's attention was drawn away from Reverend Lloyd, who stood perspiring as if he stood in a furnace, and back to Hutch.

Yet before she could even blink, he reached out, taking her face between his two powerful hands and pulling her toward him as his mouth met hers in a fierce kiss of mingled anger and desperation.

"All right, everyone out!" Doctor Swayze ordered suddenly. "I want no one else in this room while this baby is delivered." He looked to Calvin, adding, "No one but you, Calvin, and of course Mrs. Swayze."

Evangeline watched as Hutch stood and then leaned down, kissing his sister on the forehead.

"You take care of her, Hutch," Jennie panted.

"I will, Jen," Hutch promised. "But you take care of that baby. You get that baby out, and you live through it! Do you hear me?"

Jennie nodded as tears of fear and pain streamed down her face.

"Come on, Reverend," Hutch said, taking hold of Reverend Lloyd's arm in one hand and

Evangeline's in the other and pulling them out of the room.

The door closed just as Jennie wailed in agony.

"Do not push, Mrs. McKee!" Evangeline heard Doctor Swayze command. "Not until I tell you."

"I-I should probably stay . . . in case I'm needed for . . . well, anything else," Reverend Lloyd ventured.

"She'll be fine," Hutch mumbled. He leaned back against one wall a moment before sliding down into a sitting position. Jones was quick to go to his master, licking his face with an affectionate kiss of encouragement.

Evangeline was stunned—so stunned that she could think of nothing else but her proper manners. Jennie had a guest, after all—Reverend Lloyd— and the man looked as completely out of his element as a man could possibly look.

"M-might I offer you a piece of cake, Reverend Lloyd?" Evangeline asked, brushing tears from her cheeks. "I made one just this morning, and a little sweet thing goes a long way to settling one's nerves, I find."

Reverend Lloyd seemed to sense Evangeline's need for distraction. Therefore, as Jennie cried out in agony from behind the bedroom door, Reverend Lloyd said, "That would be good, I think, Miss . . . rather, Mrs. LaMontagne."

Reverend Lloyd cleared his throat, and Hutch looked up at the awkward-seeming man. Oh, he hadn't missed the reverend's obvious reminder that Hutch had just taken Evangeline to wife— even if it had been under curious and very traumatic circumstances. How could he forget such a thing! In what were perhaps her dying moments, his sister had given him what he had wanted most: Evangeline.

The truth was, Hutch was awed that Evangeline had agreed to marry him. Yet he knew how much Evangeline loved Jennie—loved her enough to grant her last request to marry him.

He nodded to Reverend Lloyd, an unspoken acknowledgement that Hutch was in his right mind and knew the magnitude of what had just transpired. But when Reverend Lloyd turned and followed Evangeline into the kitchen, Hutch wasn't so certain that *she* understood the enormity of it. After all, she'd married him as seemingly willingly as he married her, but he suspected it was different for Evangeline. For only that morning, Hutch had confided to his sister his growing feelings for her friend. Yet he doubted that Evangeline felt the same for him. Otherwise she would've confided in Jennie as well, and Jennie would have told him.

And so he wondered, as he sat with his dog's head in his lap, stroking the canine's soft head—

as he watched Evangeline serve Reverend Lloyd a piece of cake. He wondered if Evangeline had truly meant to marry him or if she thought it was all just a farce for Jennie's comfort's sake. And what would happen when Jennie's baby was born and all was well? Would Hutch simply scoop Evangeline up and carry her back to his house, over the threshold, and to their wedding bed? Surely not! Evangeline Ipswich would never have thought of that—at least not yet—not with Jennie crying out with pain in the other room.

And what if the unimaginably worst happened? What if Jennie were lost in childbirth? Would Evangeline stay with Hutch then? Remain his wife? Live with him in Red Peak simply because she'd promised her dead friend that she would? Hutch certainly did not want Evangeline's companionship for the sake of pity and obligation.

"Another push, Mrs. McKee," Hutch heard Doctor Swayze instruct. "When you feel the pain begin, push as hard as you can . . . with all your might and strength."

Hutch closed his eyes and listened—listened to his sister growl with agony and the exertion of attempting to push another human being from her body, with the attempt to bring new life into the world—and he prayed for hers to be spared.

"Hutch?" Evangeline asked in her beautiful, lilting voice.

Hutch opened his eyes to see Evangeline hunkered down in front of him, offering a glass of water to him.

"And this is for you, Jones," she said, placing a bowl of water near Jones.

Hutch took the glass from her and mumbled, "Thank you."

Jennie cried out, and Evangeline clenched her eyes tightly shut. "She'll be all right. She has to be all right," she whispered.

Hutch knew his time for weakness was over. Patting Jones on the head with reassurance, Hutch stood, took Evangeline's hand, and pulled her to her feet.

"She'll be fine," he said, attempting to appear certain. Evangeline was his wife now, and he was her husband—her protector, her provider, her companion, and perhaps one day her lover. He would be strong for her sake—no matter what the outcome eventually was on the other side of Jennie and Calvin's bedroom door.

Evangeline's hand clenched tight where Hutch held it as she heard an earsplitting, agonizing scream from Jennie's room. For a moment following Jennie's shriek, there was silence. And then, she heard it. Hutch heard it too. Even Reverend Lloyd abandoned his plate of cake to hurry toward them.

As the baby's cry broke the horrid silence

122

following Jennie's screams, a measure of comfort washed over Evangeline.

"The baby is here," she whispered to Hutch. As the baby continued to cry, a nervous giggle rose in her throat, and she repeated, "It's got a powerful set of lungs too!"

Hutch smiled a little, but Evangeline knew the worry that was still in his heart—for it was in hers too.

"And Jennie?" he asked.

Evangeline wanted to throw her arms around his neck in that moment—hold him close to her—draw strength from the power of his body and lend him the strength of the hope in her soul. But she didn't. She simply said, "I'm . . . I'm sure all is well, or they would've come for us. Wouldn't they have?"

The bedroom door opened then. Jones leapt to his three legs and began wagging his tail as Calvin stepped from the room with his and Jennie's baby swaddled in a blanket.

"It's a girl," Calvin whispered almost reverently. "A strong and healthy baby girl." He chuckled as he studied the tiny baby in his arms. "She'll need a good bath, of course," he said. "But I thought you both should know that the baby is fine."

Evangeline exhaled one sigh of relief. Yet she felt that another was waiting in its wake.

As Hutch kissed the new baby's small head and

then the fingers on one tiny hand, he asked, "And Jennie?"

Calvin gulped—seemed to force a smile. "She's . . . she's unconscious and not well. But she's alive."

Evangeline glanced past Calvin into the bedroom. She could see Jennie lying on the bed, eyes closed, as Mrs. Swayze removed some blood-soaked towels and Doctor Swayze dabbed her head with a cloth.

The baby fussed a bit and the nervous new father, Calvin, handed her to Evangeline.

"The baby will need to nurse soon," Doctor Swayze said as he walked to where Evangeline and the others stood. He looked to Evangeline and added, "I'm afraid you'll have to see to nursing the baby, Miss . . . Mrs. LaMontagne."

"Me?" Evangeline gasped.

"How is that possible, Doctor?" Hutch asked, obviously as astonished as was Evangeline.

Doctor Swayze, tired as he obviously was, chuckled all the same. "No, no, no," he began. "You'll need to be sure that the baby nurses even if Mrs. McKee isn't conscious every time."

"Oh!" Evangeline sighed with relief.

"But she will regain consciousness, won't she, Doc?" Calvin asked.

Doctor Swayze nodded. "Yes. Yes, she will. But she's lost more blood than is normal and is again with fever. I'm not sure what is wrong, so we'll have to wait it out and see if I can tell more when she's recovered for a few hours and awake."

Evangeline's second sigh of relief was not exhaled—for it was certain that Jennie was not as well as she should be.

"I'll need some warm water to bathe her in," Mrs. Swayze said as she approached. The woman smiled at Evangeline, and Evangeline could see the woman's relief in the fact that the baby, at least, was well. Her warm brown eyes conveyed it perfectly.

"I'll get that," Calvin volunteered.

"And I'll stay through the night with you, Mrs. LaMontagne," Mrs. Swayze said to Evangeline. "Just in case you need help getting her fed."

"Thank you," Evangeline said, and she was sincerely grateful—for she couldn't imagine how in the world she would get the baby to nurse if Jennie remained unconscious!

"I'll be here a while longer, as well," Doctor Swayze said. "So fear not. You're not alone in this. It's good that you have one another all the same. You may all be in for some long days and nights if Mrs. McKee doesn't recover. I mean, of course, if she doesn't recover readily." He returned to Jennie then, again pressing a cloth to her forehead.

"Well, I think my job's done here," Reverend Lloyd said. "Thank the Lord," he chuckled nervously. He reached out, shaking Calvin's hand.

125

"Congratulations, Calvin, on your new daughter. And my prayers are with your lovely wife . . . though I'm certain she will recover perfectly."

"Thank you, Reverend," Calvin said.

Reverend Lloyd turned to Evangeline then. He looked from her to Hutch and back, saying, "And congratulations to you too, Mr. and Mrs. LaMontagne. A wedding and a new baby . . . all in the same night!" He chuckled again. "I'm quite overwhelmed with joy myself." He smiled and turned toward the door. "I'll see myself out, but be sure to collect me if there's any further need of my services or company."

"I'll start heating up that water now, Mrs. Swayze," Calvin said then.

As he headed for the kitchen, Evangeline stood rather stunned. "Did he really marry us then?" she asked Hutch. "Legally? I mean, Jennie isn't . . . she'll recover. The baby and Jennie will . . . you only married me because you thought . . . we all thought . . . Jennie thought . . ."

Hutch gazed at her a moment, saying, "We married in front of God and everyone, Evangeline." He pressed his finger to the baby's palm and smiled when she clasped it. Then he looked at Evangeline again; his face was so close to hers that she could feel his sweet breath on her lips. His dark eyes fairly smoldered with the powerful allure he owned—*and* with an infallible determination. "And besides," he continued, "I'd

126

like to think I'm at least a little step up from that old poet back in Meadowlark Lake. Hmm?"

Evangeline stood awestruck, shocked into silence.

"Come along, Mrs. LaMontagne," Mrs. Swayze said then. "Let's see if we can get this little princess feeding while her daddy warms up her bath water."

Taking Evangeline's elbow, Mrs. Swayze led her and the baby into the bedroom with Jennie, closing the door behind them.

CHAPTER EIGHT

Day after day and night after night, Evangeline stayed at Jennie's bedside. When she wasn't taking care of the baby while Jennie vacillated between consciousness and deep sleep, she was taking care of Jennie—feeding her broth or soup, sponging the perspiration from her face, or reading to her to keep her calm and soothed.

Calvin and Hutchner helped as much as they could when they weren't working, rocking or walking the floors with the baby when she was fussing or reading to Jennie in turn. But Calvin needed to keep his position and resulting salary at the lumber mill, and Hutch had the livery to run. Therefore, Evangeline was left to tend to mother and child all day and through the night.

Calvin had taken up residence in Evangeline's small bed in the spare bedroom so that he might be able to sleep comfortably and be able to work the next day. It helped Evangeline as well to have Calvin in the spare room—for that way, when fatigue overtook her, she could just cradle the baby in her arms, curl up on the warm, thick rug before the hearth fire or next to Jennie on the bed, and capture a few restful moments here and there.

Still, fatigue was fast overtaking her. Furthermore, though Jennie was improving, Doctor Swayze had explained to Calvin, Evangeline, and Hutch that she "wasn't out of the woods yet" and that they needed to be very watchful of her, even yet.

The truth was that Evangeline had never experienced such thoroughgoing fatigue. And even though she loved Jennie and her baby girl with all her heart and soul, she felt a great wave of relief wash over her when, a week after the baby was born, Calvin arrived home from the lumber mill one evening with a telegram from his mother.

"Mother is on her way!" Calvin exclaimed as he entered the house that night. "Her train left Boston today, and she should arrive in two more days' time. She's going to take the train straight through to Red Peak." Going to Evangeline, he said, "I know you're worn to the bone, Evie, and I so want you to have some rest from all this— but I truly do not know what we would've done if you hadn't come to us."

"Me neither," Jennie said quietly.

Evangeline had been sitting at the foot of the bed, sharing slow and tranquil conversation with Jennie while the baby slept in her arms. And though the thought of reprieve caused her to want to burst into tears of joy and hope, she forced a smile and said, "I'm not sure I can leave you to someone else's care, Jen . . . even Calvin's mother. I've grown so accustomed to being with you both all the time." She gazed at the little bundle from heaven that Jennie weakly held in her arms. "And I'm not sure I can give up my little angel, ever!"

"You've done more than I ever had any right to ask, Evie," Jennie said.

"Yes," Calvin agreed, sitting on the bed beside his wife and nodding to Evangeline. "And it's why Jennie and I have decided to name the baby Evie . . . after you. Evie Glorietta McKee," he finished.

It was then that tears did fill Evangeline's eyes and escape to moisten her cheeks. "I-I don't know what to say," she whispered, overwhelmed with humble emotion. "I certainly do not deserve such an honor."

"Yes, you do," Hutch said.

Evangeline turned to look at Hutch—couldn't help but sigh at the handsome, alluring sight of him leaning against the doorframe.

"You've been essential, Evie," he said. "None of us could've endured this without you. Especially Jennie and little Evie."

Evangeline watched Hutch stride into the room and take little Evie in his arms when Jennie offered her to him. She watched him kiss the baby's soft brow, smile at her, and begin gently bouncing her in the cradle of his powerful arms.

Evangeline's heart fluttered, as it always did

when she looked at Hutch. Her stomach flip-flopped, as it always did when he was near. For a moment, she thought of the fact that she and Hutch were married. No one had mentioned the fact again—not in the whole week since little Evie was born—and as she always did when she set eyes on him, Evangeline wondered what would happen when Jennie and the baby didn't need her constant care anymore. And with Calvin's mother on her way to Red Peak, it seemed she would soon find out.

Would she really live as Hutch LaMontagne's wife? Would she really never go home to live again in Meadowlark Lake with her father, Kizzy, and Shay? What would she do? Would she simply begin keeping house and cooking meals for Hutch instead of Calvin and Jennie?

Yet, most of the time, Evangeline found her mind and body too tired to think on the situation very long or very deeply. She was in a constant state of secretly wishing she could just lie down and sleep until her body awoke on its own, and not because the baby was crying or Jennie calling for her. What she wanted most, however, was to fall asleep in Hutch's strong arms, to sleep there until her body and mind were rested, and then to wake up and have him kiss her again—kiss her with the power and emotion he'd kissed her with when Reverend Lloyd had stammered, "You m-may kiss the bride," an entire week past.

"My mother is a good woman, Evangeline," Calvin offered, drawing Evangeline back to the conversation at hand. "She'll take good care of Jennie and the baby. I promise you won't have to worry about them. Still, I'm hoping you'll stay, being that Mother may need her rest here and there too."

"But . . . but won't your mother need to stay in the spare room?" Evangeline asked, dizzy from fatigue. "I can't stay in there, for she'll need the space."

"Well, you'll be sleeping with me," Hutch explained. "I'll finally get to take my wife home with me."

And there it was: the answer to so many questions that had been popping around in Evangeline's tired mind, another affirmation that Hutch did truly plan to keep her as his wife, just as he'd said the night little Evie was born. Still, one thing worried her near to nausea: the fact that Hutch had not chosen to marry of his own free will, that he hadn't wanted to marry her. He'd done it only for Jennie's sake.

"She's worn right through," Hutch told Calvin as he studied Evangeline resting on the bed next to Jennie. "I'm worried that your mother might not get here in time . . . that Evangeline will take ill before deliverance arrives."

"Me too," Calvin agreed. "But Jennie and the

baby are asleep for now. Maybe they'll both sleep through the night so Evangeline can rest."

"I hope so," Hutch mumbled as he watched Evangeline sleep. He was extremely concerned for the raven-haired beauty. As far as he could tell from what she'd said, she hadn't had a full hour of uninterrupted sleep since little Evie was born, and he could see lack of good sleep was taking its toll. Evangeline was pale with dark circles under her eyes. The usual emerald brilliance of her deep green eyes had dulled, and her eyelids were constantly drooping, begging for sleep. Having Calvin's mother come to care for Jennie and the baby would indeed save Evangeline from further duress, but she was still two days away from arriving.

"The livery will just have to do without me tomorrow," Hutch said to Calvin.

Calvin looked to Hutch, frowned, and asked, "How can it do without you?"

"I'll see if I can hire one of the boys in town to tend it for me," Hutch explained. "He can always run and fetch me if something needs my attention specifically. But Evangeline needs some real rest. So I'll stay up with Jennie and the baby tonight, and . . ." He looked to Calvin, straightened his posture, and said, "Hell! I don't need to hire anyone for the livery. I can stay up tonight and work tomorrow. It won't matter if I'm a little drowsy at the livery, but you need to be at your best working with those saws and things you do at the lumberyard. What we don't need is you losing a finger or an arm because you're not at your best." Hutch frowned as realization and guilt began to overwhelm him. "I should've been helping more at night all along."

Calvin slapped a hand on Hutch's shoulder. "You have been helping at night, Hutch. Don't belittle what you've done. You've gone without a good night's sleep yourself since the baby came."

"Not enough," Hutch mumbled, disgusted with himself for allowing Evangeline to carry most of the burden. Then again, there were things that only a woman could attend to, or should attend to, where Jennie's care was concerned.

There was a soft knock on the door.

"Hello, Mr. McKee," Mrs. Swayze greeted as Calvin opened the door. "I've come to stay with Jennie and the baby tonight, if that's all right with you. Patrick and I saw Mrs. LaMontagne in the general store today when she came in for supper fixings, and she looked as limp as a dishcloth. So Patrick and I agreed I should come."

Calvin smiled. "Oh, we couldn't impose like that, Mrs. Swayze," Calvin began, though Hutch could see the relief on his face.

"Oh, nonsense!" Mrs. Swayze said, stepping into the house. "I usually do help new mothers the first few nights anyway. It was just, since

135

Mrs. LaMontagne was here, I wasn't needed. At least not until today."

Bustling into Jennie's bedroom, Mrs. Swayze set down the small carpetbag she'd brought with her and said, "I'll just stay the night in here with Jennie and the baby, and there'll be no worries for you gentlemen, all right?"

She was a bossy thing, Hutch noted. At least when her husband wasn't present.

"Well, I . . . I guess that's that then," Calvin stammered, uncertain of how else to respond.

Turning to address Hutch then, Mrs. Swayze said, "You best go ahead and take Mrs. LaMontagne home, Mr. LaMontagne. She looks plum worn out to me."

Going to the side of the bed where Evangeline was sleeping, Hutch placed a hand on her shoulder and quietly said, "Evie? Wake up."

"Me?" Evangeline asked groggily as her eyes opened.

"Mrs. Swayze has come to care for Jennie and the baby for the night, so let's get home, all right?"

"What?" Evangeline asked as sudden realization snapped her to complete and aware consciousness. She looked from Mrs. Swayze to Hutch and back. "But . . . but I can't leave Jennie," she explained. "I can't leave the baby. They'll both need to be fed and kept warm and—"

136

"That's why I'm here now, Mrs. LaMontagne," Mrs. Swayze said.

Evangeline looked to where Calvin sat in the rocking chair next to Jennie's bed. He was cradling the new baby in his arms, rocking her, and humming as he studied her tiny face and hands.

"I'll see to everything tonight," Mrs. Swayze assured Evangeline. "You've got to be completely wrung out, dear." She looked to Hutch, adding, "You too, Hutch." Patting the back of Evangeline's hand, she continued, "Now you take this handsome husband of yours on home so you both can get some sleep. You can come over and see to Jennie and the baby tomorrow. All right?"

Evangeline nodded. The truth was that she was suddenly overwhelmed with fatigue once more—both physical and emotional.

"Are you sure Jennie and the baby will be all right?" she asked.

"The baby is thriving wonderfully," Mrs. Swayze answered. "And rest and recuperation will see Jennie through, Mrs. LaMontagne. I'm sure of it." She smiled and repeated, "You go on home with your husband and get some rest."

"My husband?" Evangeline breathed. All at once, she felt dizzy. Turning to look at Hutch, she asked, "We're really married?"

Hutch's dark brows puckered with concern. "Of course, Evangeline. Are you all right?"

"Oh, the color has drained from her face completely!" she heard Mrs. Swayze exclaim.

"Hutch?" Evangeline whispered as the room seemed to begin to spin. "I think . . . I think I might . . ."

"Come on, sugar," Hutch said, swooping Evangeline up in the cradle of his arms. "Let's get you home."

Even for her dizzy, overpoweringly fatigued state, Evangeline noticed how incredibly strong Hutch was—how muscular his chest and shoulders felt as he carried her. She tried to keep her head up but couldn't help allowing it to rest on his shoulder. She could smell the skin of his neck—the warm scent of leather and linen that clung to him—and it comforted her instantly.

"Here," Mrs. Swayze said, and Evangeline felt a warm shawl being draped over her. "Get her home and warmed up, Hutch," the woman instructed. "She needs a tall glass of water and a long rest. That goes for you too."

"I-I can walk," Evangeline stammered. But when she told her body to try to escape Hutch's arms and stand, not one muscle or nerve in her would obey.

"Get that door for me, would you please, Mrs. Swayze?" Hutch asked.

"Of course," Mrs. Swayze agreed. She hurried to the front door and opened it. Hutch carried

138

Evangeline out of Calvin and Jennie's house and onto the boardwalk.

"Thank you, Mrs. Swayze," Hutch called over one shoulder.

"Of course, Mr. LaMontagne. I'm more than happy to help," Mrs. Swayze called after them.

"I-I can't possibly stay with you at your house, Hutch," Evangeline mumbled. She was still dizzy. In fact, she felt as if unconsciousness were just a wink away. "It's not proper."

"Oh, hell, Evangeline. It's entirely proper," Hutch grumbled.

CHAPTER NINE

By the time they'd reached Hutch's house, the cold evening air had drawn Evangeline from her dizzy, confused state.

"Y-you can put me down now, Hutch," she stammered as Hutch stepped up onto the front porch of his home. Naturally, she loved being cradled in his strong, capable arms, and in truth, she never wanted him to put her down. Still, she didn't want to be any more a burden than she already was. After all, Hutch now had a wife he hadn't chosen for himself.

"Not yet," he said, however. "A man has to carry his new wife over the threshold . . . or so I've heard."

Sure enough, Hutch did indeed open the front door of his house and carry Evangeline over the threshold before letting her feet gently drop to the floor and releasing her. Jones trotted in after them, sitting down in front of Evangeline and panting with obvious pleasure at her being there.

"Well, sugar," Hutch said, "welcome home." He smiled at her, stretched his arms out at his sides, and added, "It's not much, but it's sturdy and only two years old. I built it myself."

Hutch's second revelation truly impressed Evangeline. Looking around at the house's

141

interior, she noted how bright and fresh everything looked—from the kitchen to her right to the quaint parlor to her left.

"There's a woman's touch in here," she commented, as anxious suspicion began to rise in her.

"Yep," Hutch confirmed. "Jennie's."

Evangeline sighed with relief and smiling said, "I can see it now. It's very similar in furnishings as Calvin and Jennie's home."

"That's because Jennie picked out everything for me—the sofa, the rugs, the chairs," Hutch explained. "Of course, me and Calvin built the kitchen table and chairs ourselves . . . and the bed frame in the bedroom." He paused a moment and then added, "Why don't you go on in and rest a bit? I'll get a fire going in there . . . a small one so you won't be too warm." He took Evangeline by the shoulders, turning her to face him. "However, Mrs. Swayze was adamant that you drink a big glass of water before you do anything else." He winked and continued, "And the outhouse is out back." He nodded toward the back of the house. "There's a door right through there."

Evangeline blushed. She couldn't believe a man other than her father was directing her to such things as an outhouse.

Hutch could see Evangeline's discomfort. She was as red as a summer tomato. He understood that she had a lot to take in—and that she was nowhere near ready to be married to him in every physical sense of the word.

And so he said, "Why don't you drink your glass of water, and do whatever else you feel you need to do, and then just skip on into the bedroom and rest a while? I'm going to run back over to Calvin's and collect your trunk. All right?"

"A-all right," she stammered nervously.

Taking her by the shoulders again, he gazed directly into her beautiful deep-green eyes and said, "You need some rest, Evangeline. We all do. Don't worry about anything else. Do you understand what I mean?"

Her blush increased, but she smiled and nodded at him. "I am very tired," she admitted. "I don't think I've ever been this tired before . . . not in all my life."

"Well, you've good reason," Hutch said. "I'll get a little fire going in the bedroom, and you drink that glass of water Mrs. Swayze insisted on."

Her smile broadened as she looked at him, and for a moment he almost thought she was looking at him . . . well, rather lovingly. Still, Hutch knew it was foolhardy to hope too much that Evangeline would just accept that she was married to him and settle right into a life of wedded bliss. He had to be patient.

Oh, certainly he wanted nothing more in all the world at that moment than to swoop her up in his arms, carry her to what was now *their* bedroom, kiss her until her lips bruised, and consummate their marriage right then and there! But if he wanted Evangeline to love him one day, Hutch knew he was going to need more patience than he'd heretofore ever exerted collectively in his whole life!

He released his hold on her—though unwillingly, for he liked touching her—and headed toward the back of the house and the bedroom. "You get to drinking that glass of water now, you hear me?"

"I will," she called after him. Hutch could hear the happy lilt to her voice, and it encouraged him. Once he'd set the fire in the hearth in the bedroom, he'd hightail it back to Calvin's for an hour or so and let Evangeline truly rest. He figured if he waited long enough for her to slip into a deep sleep, she'd never notice that she had to share a bed with him. Hutch determined that he'd keep to his own side of the bed—even though the want and need to hold her in his arms as she slept would be almost impossible to deny. Still, he'd do it—for he did so desperately want her to fall in love with him one day—to truly *want* to be his wife—and to maybe one day thank Jennie for begging her to marry him.

Hutch had just finished getting the fire going well when Evangeline appeared at the bedroom door. Turning to look at her, he felt his breath catch in his throat. She'd unpinned her hair and was standing in the doorway combing the ebony silk with her fingers.

"The fire's going," he said, rising to his feet.

Jones trotted in at that moment, wagging his tail so hard that Hutch wondered how the three-legged dog was keeping his balance.

"Um . . . Jones is pretty used to sleeping at the foot of the bed," Hutch explained. "But I can take him with me to Calvin's if you like so he won't bother you."

Evangeline hunkered down and began scratching Jones under his jowls.

"Oh, goodness no!" she giggled. "He can keep my feet warm."

Hutch grinned. It was just another of the many things he liked about the woman—the fact that she was accepting of and affectionate with his dog. She was more than accepting, in fact. Hutch could tell Evangeline already adored Jones.

"Well, all righty then," Hutch said, standing and brushing past Evangeline as he left the room. "It's all yours. Sleep tight, now." He grinned at the beautiful woman standing in his bedroom. "Sweet dreams."

"You mean, green beans," Evangeline giggled.

"What?" Hutch asked, confused.

"Oh, it's just something my little sister Shay always says," she explained as she sat down on the bed and began to unlace her shoes. "When

her right. In the glowing firelight in the room, she could easily make out the silhouette of Hutch's broad shoulders. He was lying on his right side, facing away from her, but even for the low light, she could see that he wasn't wearing a shirt! Hutch was lying next to her on the bed with the bare skin of his back and shoulders only inches away!

Frantically covering her eyes with her hands, Evangeline gasped aloud, "Hutchner! What are you doing?"

She heard a low moan of fatigue—felt him turn onto his back as he said, "Trying to get some damn sleep, Evangeline. What're *you* doing?"

"But you're in bed with me!" she exclaimed. "And you're naked!"

Hutch roused then, and Evangeline felt him pull her hands from her eyes. There he was, leaning over her, in all his magnificent, handsome, alluring glory! His hair was mussed from sleeping, and Evangeline adored the fact so much that she almost smiled. Still, as he continued to hover over her, his eyes narrowed with weariness, she began to tremble. He was so near to her! In fact, the bareness of his chest and stomach were brushing against the day dress she still wore, but she'd broken out in such a rash of goose bumps she quivered a moment.

"I'm not naked," he said, gazing down into her eyes. He grinned a little. "My mama broke me of that habit when I was about fourteen. She said it wasn't proper." He tugged at the covers at his waist, lifted them, and said, "See? I'm wearing my long underpants."

"Oh my!" Evangeline gasped again, once more covering her eyes.

"What woke you up, sugar?" Hutch asked. He ran a hand over her arm, and even through the sleeve of her dress, the gesture caused butterflies to swarm in her stomach. "Here," Hutch said then. "I'll keep you warm. Now let's get back to sleep, hmm?"

Before Evangeline had any chance to move, Hutch reached out, laying his strong, warm, *bare* arm across her shoulders. "Turn back over. We'll be warmer that way," he mumbled. "I'm still wrung out."

Evangeline did indeed turn back to her left side, trying not to gasp when Hutch's strong arm pulled her back against him. He adjusted the covers so that her shoulders were now protected from the frigid night, but when his arm settled at her waist, Evangeline thought she might fly apart with sudden desire and delight!

She could feel his breath in her hair as he said, "Good night, Evangeline. String beans."

Evangeline smiled, thinking how adorable it was that he'd attempted to offer her family's nighttime endearment to her. "String beans," she whispered, knowing she would never sleep

149

another wink that night. How could she, with Hutch's arm around her, with his breath so warm and titillating in her hair? Maybe he really didn't mind so much that he hadn't had his choice of wife. After all, men were vastly different than women. Maybe men didn't care so much who they were married to, as long as they had a wife they could . . .

But she didn't want to think that! She wanted Hutch to want *her* and only her! She wanted him to love her the way she'd always loved him, and she especially wanted him to love her the way she'd discovered she loved him since arriving in Red Peak. She wanted him to be *in* love with her.

It didn't take long for Hutch's breathing to become slow and regular once more. When she was quite certain he was asleep, Evangeline slowly moved her right arm so that it lay on his that held her. His skin was so warm and smooth. She could feel the heat of his skin against her back where his chest was flush with her, and again goose bumps traveled over her arms and legs.

This was more than she'd ever dreamed of! The sensation of being so close to Hutch—of being held by him, of lying against him—it was euphoric! She desperately wanted to roll over and face him, kiss him directly on the mouth— wishing that he would kiss her back. But she didn't want to appear to be a wanton woman.

For pity's sake! If he thought Heather Griffiths was brazen, what would he think of Evangeline if she endeavored to seduce him into kissing her? And in *bed* of all places! He'd probably think she belonged in a saloon, rather than in his bed.

Therefore, Evangeline decided to bide her time—to be patient. Of course, she would do everything she could think of to win Hutch—to make him one day glad he had been forced to marry her. She just needed to be patient—patient, serving, and attentive. Then maybe one day, sometime in the distant future, she really would win Hutchner LaMontagne's heart for her own—just the way she'd dreamt of for as long as she could remember.

CHAPTER TEN

As the inviting aroma of sausage and warm biscuits filled his nostrils, Hutch stretched where he lay in bed. In truth, he was pretty darn surprised he'd been able to fall asleep after having been awakened by Evangeline in the middle of the night—especially since he'd been allowed to hold her, for the sake of keeping her warm. He must've been far more worn out than he'd realized to be able to sleep at all with the beauty in his arms—her warm, curvaceous body resting against his. But, by some miracle, he had slept. And though he didn't feel as wide-awake and ready for the day as he usually did, he felt better. He hoped Evangeline felt better as well. He'd been so worried for her the night before when he'd tucked her into bed and headed for Calvin's to retrieve her trunk.

Even for his lingering lethargy, when the realization struck him that Evangeline was already up and making breakfast, Hutch hopped out of bed, pulled on his trousers and boots, and headed out the back door of the house to wash his face before facing his wife after their first night together.

The water in the rain barrel was frozen over.

153

But Hutch punched a fist through the thin layer of ice, splashing a few handfuls of frigid water on his face and taking a few swallows to revive himself. If he hadn't been wide awake a moment before, he certainly was now!

Having made a quick trip to the outhouse, he paused before the mirror in the mudroom at the back of the house to run his fingers through his hair a few times, snapped his suspenders that were hanging at his waist over his shoulders, and headed into the kitchen.

In being honest with himself, Hutch was a bit nervous about facing Evangeline. She'd been so stunned to find him in bed next to her that he feared she would be angry with him. Still, she had allowed him to keep her warm, and he figured that was a good sign she didn't hate him or anything.

As he entered the kitchen and saw her standing at the stove turning some sausages in a skillet, Hutch smiled and exhaled a sigh of admiration. For a moment, he was doubtful that he was really seeing what he was seeing—the beautiful Evangeline, standing at *his* stove in *his* house, cooking breakfast for *him*.

But she really was there, and he wondered how long she'd been awake—for she was completely dressed and her hair coifed perfectly. Hutch smiled with amusement and unforeseen pleasure as he noticed she wasn't wearing any

154

shoes. She wasn't wearing any stockings for that matter either, and something about the fact caused Hutch's physical desires for her to escalate a hundredfold. Inhaling a deep breath of self-control, Hutch realized just how difficult it was going to be to be patient enough to win Evangeline's heart without ravaging her.

"Good morning."

The sound of Hutch's voice both startled and thrilled Evangeline. Whirling around, and nearly dropping the fork she'd been using to turn the sausage she was cooking, she gasped when she saw him standing in the kitchen wearing only his trousers and boots.

"G-good morning," she greeted, forcing a smile and praying she did not look as unsettled as she felt.

Oh my goodness, Evangeline thought as she studied Hutch quickly for a moment. His superb physique was far more intimidating in the broad light of day than it had been in the dark of midnight.

"I-I hope you don't mind sausage and biscuits for breakfast," she stammered. "I was going to make bacon and eggs . . . but then I wasn't sure whether you were still tired of—"

A knock on the door interrupted her.

Hutch frowned. "Who on earth can that possibly be?" he grumbled as he carefully peeked through one of the kitchen curtains. "Oh hell," he growled.

"Who is it?" Evangeline asked. It was obvious Hutch was not pleased with whomever it was.

"Heather Griffiths," he said in a whisper.

"Heather Griffiths?" Evangeline squeaked.

She was at once irritated. What was Heather Griffiths doing knocking on Hutch's front door? After all, whether it had been his choice or not, he was a married man now. He was *Evangeline's* man!

Hurrying to where Evangeline stood, Hutch took the fork from her hand and removed the skillet from the fire on the stove, setting them aside.

"Here," he whispered.

"What?" Evangeline inquired.

Hutch then reached out, quickly pulling a few pins from Evangeline's hair, causing it to begin cascading down around her shoulders.

"What are you doing?" Evangeline exclaimed in a whisper. Though she did not want Hutch knowing, she had spent quite a lot of time that morning before he'd awakened—quite a lot of time pinning her hair so that she might look her best when he woke.

"Shh!" Hutch shushed. The expression on his glorious countenance was that of pure mischief—though Evangeline couldn't fathom why.

Next he unbuttoned the top three buttons of

her shirtwaist collar—and then tugged at her shirtwaist, untucking it from her skirt.

"Hutchner!" Evangeline scolded. "What on earth are you doing?"

"Just go along with me, all right?" he asked. An impish grin spread across his face. "This will be fun. I promise!"

Another knock at the door, and he said, "Hurry! Unbutton a few more buttons of your shirt there."

"I will not!" Evangeline whispered.

"Come on, Evie," he almost begged. "Just give me this one moment of . . . of . . ."

"Hutchner?" came Heather Griffiths's voice from the other side of the door. "Are you home? I've just been to Jennie's and . . ."

Reaching out with impatience, Hutch tugged at the collar of Evangeline's shirtwaist, pulling hard enough that several buttons went flying across the room, exposing her neck and throat.

Evangeline gasped as Hutch winked at her and then turned and opened the door. Indeed, Heather Griffiths was standing on the porch.

"H-Hutchner?" Heather stammered. Her eyes fell to his shoulders, his chest, his stomach. After all, he stood before her shamelessly displaying the smooth, muscular curves of his torso.

"Heather?" Hutch said, feigning momentary confusion.

"Hutch . . . I've just been to Jennie's house to welcome her new baby . . . and she tells me that you . . . that you're married?" the young woman nearly screeched. "How can you be married?"

Hutch raked a hand through his dark hair and chuckled. "The Reverend Lloyd married us . . . didn't he, Evie?"

Hutch stepped aside, and as Heather Griffiths jealously studied Evangeline from head to toe, Evangeline understood exactly what he intended the young woman to think.

"Why . . . why yes, he did," Evangeline said, brushing a long strand of unpinned hair from her face. She nervously began to fiddle with the open collar of her shirtwaist. Stepping forward, she said, "Hutch and I have known each other since we were children, you realize," she explained, forcing a smile and taking Hutch's arm. "And when I came out to see Jennie . . ." She shrugged, feigning naïveté. She looked to Hutch and smiled, "Well, the moment I saw him . . . it was as if we'd never been apart."

Hutch released Evangeline's arm where she'd been holding it and instead placed his hands at her waist, turning her to face him. There was nothing she could do but place her hands on his warm, broad chest and smile at him—for Heather Griffiths's sake, of course.

"You married this woman?" Heather nearly growled.

"I did," Hutch said, placing a firm kiss to Evangeline's cheek. "I couldn't help myself.

She's so beautiful, and I've loved her for so long. And once she stepped off that train and back into my life . . ."

Evangeline startled when Heather screeched with anger and frustration. "You've ruined everything, Hutch!" the girl growled. She looked to Evangeline, hatred fairly spitting from her eyes. "Fine," she said to Hutch then. "You could've had me, Hutch. But you chose her instead. Therefore, all I can tell you is . . . well, you've made your bed, so you're the one who'll have to lie in it!"

Hutch smiled, however, saying, "Oh, I have, Heather." He looked to Evangeline, pressed a long, lingering, warm kiss to her mouth, and then said, "I have," and closed the door in Heather Griffiths's face.

Evangeline heard Heather squeal a bit with fury, stomp down the front porch steps—and then she was gone.

"You're terrible!" Evangeline scolded Hutch, though she couldn't keep from laughing. The truth was, she'd been somewhat thrilled when she'd realized just what Hutch was trying to make Heather assume. Oh, it was devilish of her to willingly play a part in his deceit, but she was glad she had.

Hutch shrugged, however. "That woman has been driving me near to drink for over a year now," he explained. His smile broadened.

"But . . . I expect she's finished with me now. Don't you?"

"I would hope so," Evangeline admitted. The truth was, she could hardly think straight! Hutch had kissed her! His warm lips pressed so firmly against hers had turned Evangeline's innards to spring-day slush. Not to mention the fact that he still held her against him—that her palms were still pressed against the warm, solid contours of his chest.

"Now wasn't that fun?" he asked her. "A little mischief always puts an extra sparkle in your eye, you know, Evie. It always has."

"Well, you're not the one who has to sew three buttons back onto this shirtwaist, now are you?" she teased.

Hutch's gaze was so mesmerizing! He was staring at her intently, rather as if he didn't plan on releasing her any time soon. The deep, cool blue of his eyes seemed to boil somehow as he looked at her. His expression thoroughly thrilled her, caused her to quiver with wanting to kiss him—to think of the bed Heather Griffiths had accused him of making—and of lying in it with him.

"Oh! I forgot to tell you," Evangeline exclaimed, however—too uncomfortable to continue with the train of thought she'd begun. Whether or not Hutch was, by law, her husband—whether or not her feelings were so strong for him that she hated every moment he was away from her, longed to be in his arms with every breath she took—she didn't quite know how to surrender to his teasing implications. For always in the back of her mind was the question of how sincere his teasing was.

Therefore, she casually stepped out of his grasp and said, "I found a spider this morning—a huge, huge, enormously monstrous wolf spider—and I couldn't find the courage to step on it. So I was wondering if you wouldn't mind getting rid of it for me. Otherwise, I'll never be able to sleep again, you know."

Hutch shook his head and chuckled, obviously amused. "That's what you're thinking about right now, Evangeline?" he asked. "We just sent one of our neighbors off into the world thinking scandalous thoughts of what you and I are up to in here . . . and you want me to kill a spider for you?"

Evangeline nodded. "If you wouldn't mind," she assured him. "I abhor spiders."

Hutch sighed, chuckled again, and asked, "All right. Where's this monster spider you need squashed?"

"In the kitchen," Evangeline told him.

She was a coward! A spineless coward! She knew neither of her sisters would've backed away so hastily from the men that they loved, and it made her wonder what was wrong with her. And yet Amoretta's and Calliope's circumstances of marriage were vastly different than her own. They'd been proposed to by the men they loved, planned weddings, been married properly with many witnesses, had photographs as proof that their men loved them enough to marry them. It wasn't the same—wasn't the same as Hutch actually wanting to marry her of his own free will.

"I did manage to put an empty peach bottle over it," Evangeline explained as she followed Hutch into the kitchen. "But I swear it's so big its legs were still sticking out of the bottle rim at first."

Evangeline shivered with wild discomfort as Hutch approached the large glass jar sitting over the spider on the kitchen floor. She watched as he hunkered down in front of the jar and placed a hand on it.

"Ahhh!" Evangeline screamed, hopping up onto one of the kitchen chairs. "What are you doing? Are you insane?" She wished she'd put on her shoes before she'd dressed, for now her bare feet were at the mercy of being crawled on if the spider escaped its glass prison.

Hutch looked up at her a moment and smiled. "Well, I gotta move the jar if I'm gonna stomp the spider, sugar," he chuckled.

But as Hutch lifted the jar, the unusually large wolf spider did indeed fulfill Evangeline's fears

162

by quickly scampering across the floor toward the very chair on which she was standing.

Horror-struck, Evangeline hopped from the chair she'd been standing on onto the kitchen table, squealing and dancing about as if the table-top were a bed of hot coals instead of just an ordinary (and harmless) piece of furniture.

Even after she heard the hard stomp of Hutch's boot on the floor—even after he'd assured her the spider was dead and he'd gone to the stove to scrape its remains from his boot on the pile of wood in the wood bucket there—Evangeline's skin was swarming with the residual goose bumps, goose bumps of terror.

"My skin is crawling!" she said as she remained standing on the table. "I'll never, ever get to sleep tonight! How many other monsters like that are in here, do you think?"

Evangeline watched as Hutch turned back toward her, bending to one side as he studied something. It took her only an instant to realize he was staring at her legs—her scandalously bare feet and legs! When she'd leapt up to the chair (and then the table), she'd been clutching her skirt and petticoats, keeping the hem lifted to nearly her knees for fear another spider might appear and endeavor to scramble up her legs. Even her pantaloons had somehow managed to bunch up above her knees, so that her knees were visible as well—visible to Hutch!

Evangeline dropped her skirt and petticoats at once, properly covering her calves, ankles, and feet. Her goose bumps of terror were quickly spiraling into goose bumps of embarrassment and a scarlet blush of humiliation.

Hutch straightened to his full height, smiled, and said, "Mercy! I've never seen a woman's bare, naked legs before. It's a beautiful sight indeed . . . yes, indeed it is. At least *your* bare, naked legs are a beautiful sight." His smile broadened as he added, "I'm finding there really are quite a lot of advantages to being married to you, Evangeline."

"You are a terrible tease, Hutchner LaMontagne!" Evangeline scolded, blushing to the very core of her being. Quickly she stepped off the table, onto the chair, and then from the chair to the floor, carefully glancing about just in case any more morbid, horrifying spiders were lurking about. "You're no gentleman at all."

"What do you mean?" he asked, feigning ignorance. "I killed the spider, didn't I?" he chuckled.

"Yes, you did. And thank you," Evangeline said, nodding at him. "But you shouldn't have taken advantage of my . . . my state of undress and . . . and looked at my legs the way you did." Evangeline wondered if Hutch really did think her legs were beautiful. She certainly hoped he did. Still, a proper woman was bound by society to feign horror at having had a man see her legs.

Hutch shook his head and laughed. "Evangeline, when in the world are you gonna get it through your head that I'm your husband?" he playfully reminded her. Striding over to stand directly in front of her, he took hold of her shoulders, smiled, and said, "I'm your husband, your man . . . forever. I could stand here, strip you down to nothing, and look at you all day long if I wanted to, and no one would fault me for it."

When Evangeline gasped with astonished chagrin, Hutch simply laughed again, however, adding, "Oh, and you're more than welcome to do the same to me anytime you want."

The thought of Hutch in any more of a state of undress than he already was—usually parading around in nothing but his trousers and boots—was so startling to Evangeline that she found she couldn't speak.

Therefore, having either misunderstood her silence as approval of the idea or simply wanting to mercilessly taunt her again, Hutch said, "Just say the word, my beautiful, very blushing bride." His voice was lowered to an outrageously provocative voice. He then proceeded to unfasten his belt, strip it from his trouser waist, and toss it to the table, as well. "Just say the word, and I'll—"

"Oh my! No!" Evangeline gasped. "I swear, Hutch! What is your obsession with nudity?"

But Hutch only laughed low in his throat and

165

winked at her. "It ruffles your bloomers, honey, that's all. I like to see you bashful and nervous. You're extra delicious when you're like that—vulnerable and girly, instead of so proper the way you sometimes feel you have to be."

Even for the fact that she was so casually attired—that her hair was down and her feet bare—Evangeline straightened her posture with an air of defiance. "What do you mean? I *am* proper."

"No, you're not," Hutch countered. "You're fun and frivolous." He leaned closer and bent down until his face was level with hers. "You're passionate and playful, just like me." He straightened his own posture then. "But you weren't expecting to have to marry over my sister's deathbed the way you did. It kind of took the fun out of it for you—turned the fairy tale wedding all little girls dream about into a . . . well, sort of a mess. So I don't think it's ever really sunk into your brain that we really are husband and wife."

Evangeline found herself shaking her head, her brows arched in astonishment. "It sunk in. I mean, I'm living with you, aren't I? I wouldn't be living in your house with you, and sleeping next to you in your bed, if it hadn't sunk in."

"I don't know," he attested. "For instance," he began then. Evangeline stiffened as his hands moved to her waist—as he pulled her body against his. "Right now, you're thinking you like me. But part of you doesn't believe I'm really your husband . . . being that the reverend married us in less than a minute, in truth."

Evangeline's breath felt labored; her heart was racing like a train engine! He was so very, very handsome! So alluring—so wholly seductive! And every inch of Evangeline wanted to reach out, throw her arms around his neck, and beg him to kiss her—to love her as thoroughly as she loved him! But she just couldn't. For some reason, her body wouldn't obey her mental commands to reach out and take Hutchner LaMontagne for her own.

"I don't know much about much," Hutch said then. "But I do know a fair amount about you, Evangeline." His eyes narrowed, smoldered with mischief. "You forget that I watched you grow up from just a little thing to a young woman. And now . . . now you're a woman—full-grown, beautiful, and so enchanting as to make a man's head spin near clean off his body . . . especially mine."

Evangeline felt tears welling in her eyes. Oh, how desperately she wanted to freely express her feelings for him—to reveal the tenderness of her heart to him and let him keep it as his own!

Yet it *was* hard to believe—to believe that Hutch could care for her the way she cared for him—especially when he'd basically been forced to marry her.

Unexpectedly then, Evangeline found herself asking, "What do you want from me, Hutch?" If he just told her that all he really wanted was for her to give herself to him physically, maybe she could find a way to do that for him and still protect herself from a measure of heartache in knowing he hadn't chosen her. Maybe if he told her exactly what he did want from her, she could endeavor to win his heart and sincere affections. "Do you want me to . . . to . . ." She nodded toward their bedroom.

But Hutch suddenly took her face in his hands, gazing into her eyes with a wanton expression, yes, but also an expression of deep emotion and caring. It so startled Evangeline, and she stood stuck to the place she was, trembling with a sudden wave of desire washing over her.

"I just want you to trust me, to accept me," he mumbled against her ear. "I want you to know that I married you, willingly . . . and that I'm your husband . . . and that I want you for my wife."

Evangeline felt warm all over—warmer than she'd ever felt before in all her life. She felt her body relax a bit against his and found the courage to say, "I *do* know we're legally married, you know."

"Do you?" he asked, kissing her cheek again.

Evangeline smiled—sighed with momentary contentment.

Contentment until Hutch added, "Well then, why don't you pucker up and give me some sugar? After all, you did just admit that you know we're married. I swear, Jones gets more attention from you than I do."

"Jones does not get more attention from me than you do," Evangeline told him.

"Yes, he does," Hutch corrected, grinning at her. "You're always petting him, talking to him in that sweet voice of yours."

"Well, fine then," Evangeline said. "I'll try to give you more attention than I give to Jones, from here on out." She smiled, reached up, and patted Hutch on the top of the head.

Hutch rolled his eyes and shook his head.

"Oh, and Jones likes when I do this too," Evangeline giggled, reaching behind both of Hutch's ears and gently scratching him there. "Satisfied?" she teased.

"No," Hutch mumbled, still grinning at her.

His patience was wearing thin. And besides, Hutch could see that Evangeline cared for him. He could feel it in her touch—even the way she teasingly scratched behind his ears.

"Evangeline," he began. He couldn't keep from staring at her mouth. He'd meant to tell her what he'd been up to during the past week—about the

169

telegrams. And yet part of him wanted her to fall in love with him then and there, before he told her his plans.

"Yes?" she asked, staring up at him with an expression of invitation. But an invitation to what?

She wanted to kiss him—to fairly smother him with kisses! To be wrapped in his arms, held against his strong, warm, protective body. But she didn't know how to begin! Evangeline could see in Hutch's eyes that he did care for her. It was all so ridiculous, the discomfort she felt. She knew she could trust him and that he would eventually love her—if he didn't already. And by the expression in his beautiful eyes, she was beginning to believe that he did.

Hutch sighed, grinned a little, and said, "It'll keep."

Disappointed—for she had hoped Hutch had been about to confess to her that he loved her—Evangeline said, "Well, do you want your breakfast now?" After all, what else could she say? And she knew Hutch must be hungry.

Hutch grinned—the sort of roguish grin that caused Evangeline's heart to quiver with delight. "Yes," he said. "I do want my breakfast."

And then—oh, blessedly then—it happened. Taking her face between his hands once more, Hutchner LaMontagne kissed Evangeline—

thoroughly kissed her! In fact, his kiss was so affecting to her entire being that she was struck breathless and dizzy and simultaneously whisked into such a flurry of pleasurable emotions and physical elation that she quite thought she would faint for a moment.

This kiss was not the quick, fierce sort of kiss that Evangeline had experienced when Reverend Lloyd had pronounced her and Hutch married, nor was it the soft, lingering kiss she'd experienced from him just minutes before in front of Heather Griffiths. This kiss was wildly passionate—hot, moist, and invigorating to her very core! This kiss was driven, wanton, and busting with barely bridled emotion!

Over and over and over Hutch's mouth worked to blend with Evangeline's! And over and over and over Evangeline's worked to blend with his—until such a fever of fervor was burning between them that Evangeline thought that if the house were burning down around her, she wouldn't care—wouldn't pause their ardent exchange.

Never had Evangeline known such a kiss! Oh, she'd been witness to similar moments between her sisters and their husbands—even between her father and Kizzy. But to experience it with Hutch—oh, even her dreams of him had not been near to what the reality was!

Another knock on the door disturbed their rapture, however.

"Dammit!" Hutch growled as he released Evangeline, stormed to the door, opened it, and nearly shouted, "What?"

It was Mrs. Swayze, and her eyes bugged out like a mouse caught in a trap as she studied Hutch from head to toe.

"Oh . . . oh my!" she breathlessly exclaimed. The doctor's wife blushed, gulped, and looked past Hutch and his magnificence to where Evangeline stood behind him. "Pardon me, Mrs. LaMontagne," she began—her eyes darting back to Hutch's chest, her blush deepening. "But Patrick needs me to assist in another birthing, and I thought you might want to run over to be with Mrs. McKee and the baby while I'm gone. Though I do think she's quite on the mend. She seems more herself this morning."

Mrs. Swayze gulped again—stared at Hutch's chest once again.

"Of course," Evangeline said. "I'll go right over. Thank you, Mrs. Swayze. Thank you for everything. I really did need a good night's sleep."

"I'm sure you did," Mrs. Swayze said, hurriedly turning and fairly racing down the steps.

Knowing by the expression of frustration on Hutch's face that the passionate, loving moment between them had been ruined by Mrs. Swayze's sudden appearance and announcement that Jennie was alone, Evangeline exhaled a heavy sigh and said, "The sausage and biscuits are ready, Hutch. I'll . . . I'll run over to be with Jennie. But you enjoy breakfast, all right?"

Hutch inhaled a deep, deep breath, exhaling it slowly—an obvious attempt to not only calm himself but also accept that their morning had been interrupted.

"All right," he said. "You run over to Jennie's. I better get out to the livery." He looked to her then, adding, "But I'll be honest with you, Evangeline. I can hardly wait for Calvin's mother to get here and take over for a while."

"I know," Evangeline managed, smiling at him.

As Hutch rather stormed back toward the bedroom—mumbling, "I guess I better put on a damn shirt before any other ladies come poking around"—Evangeline giggled. The look on Mrs. Swayze's face when she'd been met at the door by an artistically chiseled, half-naked Hutchner LaMontagne had been priceless. It had almost been worth the interruption.

As Evangeline turned to head back to the bedroom herself to fetch her shoes, she wobbled—almost fell over for the sake that her knees were so weak from the lingering effects of Hutch's kiss. And she determined then and there that if Hutch felt enough for her to kiss her the way he had, then she would find a way (and soon) to break through the barrier that was her own shy insecurity and meet him tit for tat the next time

173

he kissed her. She only prayed that there would be a next time—that there would eventually be not only a next time but an every time—an all the time.

CHAPTER ELEVEN

As fate would have it, Jennie needed Evangeline both that full day and all through the night. But as anxious as Evangeline was to return with Hutch to their home, she'd tried to enjoy her time with Jennie—and she had. For one thing, Jennie had laughed so hard when Evangeline had related the stories of Heather Griffiths's and Mrs. Swayze's arrivals and what followed that Evangeline felt it was more healing for her friend than all the bed rest in the world. Furthermore, she loved helping to care for little Evie. The baby was so tender and sweet. She put Evangeline in mind of having her own sweet babies one day—babies fathered by Hutch.

There was a worry, however, concerning the arrival of Calvin's mother. Hutch and Calvin, and everyone else in Red Peak for that manner, had begun to sense the oncoming of a storm. Calvin worried for his mother—that the train would arrive during the worst of it and find him unable to fetch her home properly. And sure enough, as often happens, Calvin's concerns were justified.

On the day that Calvin's mother was to arrive, a snowstorm did descend on Red Peak. Though it wasn't a full blizzard yet, Hutch and Calvin were both certain that by the end of the day, it would be.

"I'll go for your mother," Hutch said as Evangeline rocked little Evie and watched the snow swirl outside the windows.

"I don't want you getting stuck out there, Hutch," Calvin argued, however.

"You need to be here with Jennie and the baby," Hutch explained. "I know my way even in a storm, and my team is the best in town for travel in snow. I'll take Evangeline home, and then I'll go to the station and wait for your mother."

"Evangeline can stay here," Jennie suggested. "I'd be glad for her company."

Evangeline watched, however, as Hutch inhaled a deep breath. She could tell he was irritated.

"I know, Jen," he said, calmly. "But if we're going to be snowed in for three or four days . . . well, we've all had a lot of each other these past few weeks. And with Calvin's mom coming to stay, I think it would be best for Evangeline and me to make sure we're home when the heavy snows come."

"But, Hutch, what if something happens and you don't make it back from the train station before the snow hits?" Jennie asked, obviously very worried.

Evangeline's heart dropped to the pit of her stomach. "Can that happen?" she asked, suddenly very frightened.

"Not to me," Hutch assured her.

"Are you sure, Hutch?" Calvin asked.

Hutch nodded. "I am." He turned to Evangeline and said, "Let's get you home and get the fires started, all right? I'll need some extra time to prepare the team to go to the station."

Evangeline nodded, her fear mounting. She'd read about the blizzards that often came to the area in winter. Four, five, sometimes six feet of blowing snow, with conditions that left a body unable to see past the end of his own nose. She was well aware that more than a few people had died—frozen to death—while trying to make their way home after seeing to livestock or searching for others that had lost their way in a storm. Still, she tried to appear as calm as possible.

That was until she and Hutch stepped out into the cold, blowing snow that had already arrived in Red Peak.

"Come on," Hutch said, taking Evangeline's hand. "Let's get you home before this gets any worse."

"But I want you to stay too," she told him. Still, she knew that Jennie needed Calvin to be with her, especially if the town really did find itself buried for several days. And what of Calvin's mother? The train would arrive, blizzard or not. What would become of her if Hutch didn't fetch her home to the warmth and safety of Jennie's?

"I'll be fine, Evie," he told her.

As the wind fairly blew them into the house when Hutch opened the door, Jones barked, charging past them and going right to the hearth in the parlor. Finding no fire there with which to warm himself, he barked again.

"I'll get a fire started in here," Hutch said. "Do you think you could get one going in the bedroom, so I can get that team started for the train station?"

"Of course," Evangeline assured him. She was frightened—frightened of the coming storm—frightened of Hutch going out into it.

"Jones will stay here with you," Hutch said as he placed fresh kindling on the grate in the parlor fireplace. "And I'll be back as soon as I can."

"All right," Evangeline said. She was trying to look brave—the way she'd always tried to look, ever since her mother had been lost when she was twelve years old, leaving Evangeline to be the brave oldest sister of the Ipswich family. But she wanted to be weak! She wanted to throw her arms around Hutch's neck and tell him that someone else could take care of Calvin's mother when she arrived at the station. Still, she knew that was a horrid thing to even think.

And so she stood, wringing her hands and watching as Hutchner put on a heavier pair of boots, a heavier coat, and thick gloves.

When he'd finished dressing for the weather and the fire was burning strongly in the parlor hearth, Hutch went to Evangeline, took her hands in his, and gazing down at her with fierce determination said, "I'll be back, Evangeline. And when I get back . . . we'll pick up breakfast where we left off the other morning, all right?"

She couldn't keep from smiling then—even with the peril that awaited Hutch outside.

"All right," she agreed. And how grateful and elated was she when Hutch cupped her chin in one gloved hand, pressing a solid, driven kiss to her mouth. "You keep an eye on Evangeline for me, Jones. You hear me?" Hutch called to the dog before smiling at Evangeline and leaving by way of the back door.

Jones trotted in from the parlor, depositing his hindquarters on the entryway floor at Evangeline's feet.

Evangeline smiled at the three-legged canine. "I guess we'll just have to wait this out together, won't we, Jones?" she said, reaching down to scratch the dog behind his ears. The dog barked once in agreement and then began panting happily as he stared up at her.

"He'll be fine, won't he?" Evangeline mumbled more to herself than to Jones. "He has to be fine. He has to come back to me so we can finish our breakfast . . . isn't that right?"

• • •

The snow was already torrential when Hutch finally reached the train station. The moment he saw the well-dressed Bostonian woman standing out on the station platform shivering, even for the fact she wore furs from head to toe, he knew it was a good thing he'd come for Calvin's mother.

Calvin McKee was a strong, capable man, but Hutch had far more experience with the blizzards that hit out west than he did. And the truth was, Hutch worried whether he himself and the team could find their way back to Calvin's house, let alone if Calvin had been the one trying.

"Mrs. McKee?" Hutch called through the wind and swirling snow. "Mrs. McKee? Ma'am? Are you Calvin McKee's mother, ma'am?"

"Wh-why, yes!" the woman called above the storm.

"I've come to fetch you back to Calvin and Jennie's," Hutch explained as he set the wagon break and jumped down.

"Oh, thank the Lord!" Mrs. McKee sighed. "I got off the train expecting . . . well, more than this, I suppose."

"Are these the only trunks you have, ma'am?" Hutch said, eyeing the four traveling trunks that stood on the station platform. He thought of the one small trunk Evangeline had brought with her and wondered what in all the world a woman would need four traveling trunks for.

"Yes, sir!" Mrs. McKee assured him.

"I'm Hutch LaMontagne, Mrs. McKee," he explained quickly. "Jennie's brother."

"Oh, thank you for coming for me, Mr. LaMontagne! I was quite beginning to panic."

Wasting no further time in idle conversation, Hutch loaded Mrs. McKee's trunks into the wagon. The weather was worsening by the second, and all he could think about was getting home to Evangeline. He knew she would be frightened—worried for him. What's more, he hadn't been able to forget the feel of having her in his arms—the sweet flavor of her warm mouth pressed to his. He hadn't been able to think of anything else since the moment Mrs. Swayze had interrupted them two days before. He wanted to return to her—have her all to himself—to find out if her feelings for him were more intense than he'd first thought.

And so, once Hutch had loaded Mrs. McKee's trunks into the wagon, he did not stand on ceremony. Impatiently striding to the woman, he simply swooped her up in his arms and carried her to the wagon.

"Oh my!" Mrs. McKee exclaimed. "You surely must think this storm is worsening, Mr. LaMontagne."

"It most certainly is, Mrs. McKee," Hutch said, helping her onto the wagon seat. Hopping up beside her, he added, "And besides, I know

181

how anxious you must be to see your new grand-daughter. She's named Evie, you know . . . after my wife."

"Oh, h-how wonderful!" Mrs. McKee exclaimed as Hutch slapped the lines at the team's backs, starting the wagon lurching forward.

Hutch was more driven than he'd ever been in all his life before that moment—driven to get home—driven to get back to Evangeline.

"It's been hours, Jones," Evangeline said as she stroked Jones's soft ears. "We've been sitting here for hours . . . and the storm is so much worse!" Tears filled her eyes again, as they'd been doing off and on since Hutch had left to bring Calvin's mother home from the train station.

Fears she didn't even know she had had welled up inside Evangeline's mind and heart—visions of Hutch being frozen solid and still clutching the lines of his team, also frozen solid. Thoughts of being widowed before she'd even had a chance to know her beloved Hutch as truly her husband. Yet Evangeline fought her fears as best she could. She'd even read aloud for over an hour—read poetry aloud to Jones. And although he seemed rather uninterested, it did help Evangeline to pass the time—at least for a little while.

But now—now it was long past sunset. Now the snow was so thick and heavy as it fell that she couldn't see anything at all past the windowpane.

The clock on the wall chimed eight, and the noise was more ominous than soothing, the way clock chimes normally were.

"Well, Jones, I suppose we should perhaps just ready ourselves for bed," Evangeline said. "I'm certain Hutch made it to the train station and found Calvin's mother. Perhaps, being that the snow and wind are so bad now, he just chose to wait out the storm at Jennie's, rather than risk being lost in the . . ." She gulped as terror welled in her throat. "Come on, Jones," she said. "Let's get ready for bed. I'll read to you some more then, all right?"

With fear and anxiety at full breadth, Evangeline rose from her seat in the parlor and headed for the bedroom.

With so many hours to fill while Hutch had been absent, she'd quite settled into the house by putting her things in two empty drawers she'd found in Hutch's chest of drawers in the bedroom.

Quickly, she removed her day dress and hung it on a hanger in the wardrobe. Slipping off her petticoat, shoes, and stockings, Evangeline wondered for a moment if her nightgown would be warm enough. Perhaps she should've remained in her day dress.

Evangeline gasped then as she heard the door at the back of the house blow open—heard Hutch call to her, "I'm back! Boy, oh, boy, are we in for it." He laughed and added, "A body can't see a thing out there! And it's colder than a witch's stone heart!"

Hurrying into the mudroom at the back of the house, careless of her state of undress, Evangeline watched in silence as Hutch removed his gloves, coat, and boots.

It wasn't until he turned and saw her that she allowed her tears to spill from her eyes and flood her cheeks.

"A-are you all right, Evangeline?" Hutch asked, studying her from head to toe a moment.

Having quite forgotten that she was now wearing only her pantaloons and camisole, Evangeline stomped one bare foot and sobbed, "Do you know how worried I've been, Hutch? I've been sick with worry! I thought you'd frozen to death and would never be coming home."

"But . . . I'm fine," Hutch said, his brow puckering a bit with confusion. "I told you I'd be back, and I am."

Evangeline wasn't angry with him. She was just so relieved! After having spent hours in agony, she was so relieved to see Hutch safe and back home that she was quite out of her mind for a moment.

Racing to him, she threw herself against him and continued to sob. "I thought certain you were dead! I-I imagined such horrid things, Hutch!"

She felt Hutch's strong hands at her waist—at

184

her actual waist—at her actual dressless, petticoatless, bare-skinned waist. But she didn't care about the impropriety of it, for the feel of his hands on her skin was assurance that he was there—alive and well and there. Furthermore, it was a purely blissful sensation, and it drove her emotions to even higher zeal.

"I love you! I love you! I love you, Hutch!" she confessed, burying her face against his neck—drinking in the warm, soothing scent of leather and linen that clung to it. "I've loved you ever since I can remember! And I'm sorry you were forced to marry me! I'm sorry Jennie made you marry me, Hutch. No! I'm not sorry! Because even if you don't love me the way I love you, you're mine! You're mine, do you hear me? Mine! And I don't ever want to be separated from you again! Ever!"

"But I do love you," Hutch said.

Evangeline's breath caught in her throat, and she looked up at him, brushing tears from her cheeks. "Wh-what did you say?"

Hutch grinned—that alluring, mischievous, seductive grin Evangeline so loved. "I do love you," he repeated. "I've loved you from the moment you turned around and looked at me that day at the station."

"What?" Evangeline whispered again, unable for a moment to believe him.

"And I didn't marry you because Jennie made

me," he said. "Jennie could never make me do anything I didn't want to do. I wanted to marry you . . . and I've felt guilty all this time for tricking you into it."

"But you didn't," Evangeline said. "I've wanted to marry you, always. And Jennie knew that. That's why she made you—"

"She didn't make me, Evangeline," Hutch interrupted. "I married you because I wanted you . . . because I love you."

"But you only knew me . . . you only knew me a week," she reminded him.

"I've known you for years, Evie," he reminded her in return. "You'd just grown up to be old enough for me to fall in love with you now, that's all."

He smiled, and Evangeline felt his hands move from her waist to her back. Slowly he caressed her there—on the warm, bare skin of her lower back. Goose bumps raced over her arms, her legs, her back, even her fingers, at his intimate touch.

"Now," he said, "what do you say we pick up where we left off at breakfast the other morning, hmm?"

Evangeline smiled at him, gazing into the smoldering cobalt of his eyes. She could see herself there—literally see herself in his eyes— see that he loved her—really, truly loved her.

"All right," she agreed, an uncomfortable bashfulness rising in her. After all, she was wearing

186

only her camisole and pantaloons. "I'll just put my nightgown on and—"

"Don't bother, sugar," Hutch said, however. "You're not gonna need it."

Evangeline gasped as Hutch pulled her against him, ravaging her mouth with loving, wanton kisses that sent her senses spiraling into blissful waves of surrender. Hutch loved her! He loved her! His ardent, steaming kisses were proof. His skillful caresses and the words he whispered against her mouth—all of it validated Evangeline's dreams come true! She owned Hutchner LaMontagne's heart, as fully as he owned hers.

Hutch broke the seal of their lips for a moment, and Evangeline smiled and teased, "But I promised Jones I'd read to him."

Hutch chuckled, swooped Evangeline up in his arms, and said, "Well, Jones will just have to wait." As he carried Evangeline to their bedroom, gently laying her on their bed, he added, "And it could be a long wait at that."

As shared kisses as hot as the embers smoldering in the hearth and as delicious as nectared ambrosia passed between them then, Evangeline thought of nothing but Hutch— Hutchner LaMontagne—and all the joy they would know in their life as husband and wife—as lovers—beginning that night.

EPILOGUE

As Evangeline held her two baby sisters, one in each arm, she could hardly believe it! Ever since she and Hutch had moved to Meadowlark Lake just before Thanksgiving to find that Kizzy had given birth to twin baby girls, Evangeline was amazed to think that her father now had six daughters—when less than two years before he'd only had three!

"Kizzy," she began as Hutch returned from the kitchen and clapped his hands to indicate he wanted to hold one of the twins, "I know they're real, and I know they're yours and Daddy's. But every time I look at them, I still cannot believe it . . . twins!"

Kizzy laughed. "I know what you mean, Evie," she said. "I still stand awestruck when I look at them."

"I don't," Shay said, hopping up into Evangeline's lap and kissing little Leonora's forehead. "To me they're the baby sisters I've always prayed for." Shay smiled and kissed Evangeline's cheek. "To go with the big sisters I always prayed for." Hopping from Evangeline's lap, Shay tugged on Hutch's shirttail, indicating she wanted to kiss Peanna, as well.

Hutch smiled and hunkered down, enabling Shay to kiss Peanna's forehead.

"And now," Shay announced, her dark curls bouncing this way and that as she twirled around in the new dress her mother made and gifted her for Christmas, "everybody gather round. I have prepared a performance."

"Another performance, Shay?" Brake teased as he helped Amoretta, who was expecting her first baby in just a month or so, take a seat on the sofa in the parlor.

"Yes, Uncle Brake," Shay said. "Another performance . . . and this is one you'll really love!"

"I'm sure we'll love it, Shay Shay," Rowdy said as he pulled Calliope to sit on his lap in sharing his chair.

"Daddy," Shay began, "will you please hold Leonora and Peanna for me? They'll need to be with you during part of the performance."

"Of course, honey," Lawson Ipswich agreed with a chuckle.

Evangeline and Hutch both handed the babies off to Lawson before taking a seat on the floor at the foot of the sofa.

Evangeline admired her father's patience with their little sister. In fact, the more she thought of it, the more she realized that their father had more patience and understanding with Shay than anyone else.

Shay's marmalade cat meowed from her place

on the rug in front of the hearth fire, and Shay snapped her fingers, calling, "Jones? Jonesie? Molly wants company, please."

Hutch mumbled with amusement, "That child amazes me with that dog of ours, Evie."

"She certainly is a wonder with animals," Evangeline agreed.

"She's a wonder with people too," Hutch quietly chuckled. "Look at all of us here, just waiting and willing to do her bidding."

"I know," Evangeline giggled.

"Mama, you sit there next to Daddy and the babies," Shay instructed.

"I will, darling," Kizzy agreed. Then lowering her voice, she added, "But be mindful of being too bossy, all right?"

"Yes, Mama," Shay agreed, blushing with a having been slightly reprimanded. "But I promise all of you . . . you will love this performance."

Everyone laughed and watched as Shay produced a wooden box from under the sofa. "Quiet down now, quiet down. I'm about to begin."

Everyone did as instructed, and Hutch whispered to Evangeline, "I do find her performances very entertaining. I can't wait for Jennie to see one when she and Calvin finally get down here."

"Oh, Jennie will love Shay!" Evangeline exclaimed in a whisper. "Those two will be fast friends, I know it."

The room went quiet as Shay opened the

wooden box and retrieved a cabinet card. Clearing her throat, the dark-haired, wide-eyed angel began to sing, "There were three little girls dressed in blue." Whirling about in her new red Christmas dress, Shay offered the cabinet card that Evangeline recognized as Amoretta and Brake's wedding photograph to Amoretta. As Amoretta accepted the cabinet card, Shay whispered, "Hold it up so everyone can see, Amoretta."

With an entertained giggle of delight, Evangeline's beautiful, brown-haired sister held up her wedding photograph for everyone to see, at which point Shay bowed low before Amoretta and sang, "Then one married and left only two."

Taking another cabinet card from the box, Shay whirled over to Calliope, offering it to her. Evangeline's striking blonde-haired, blue-eyed little sister smiled and held up her wedding photograph for everyone to see as Shay sang, "Then one fell in love with a boy . . . who loved her and gave her much joy."

Everyone chuckled when Rowdy mumbled, "Boy?" feigning offense.

Going to the box once more, Shay removed one more cabinet card, whirled over to Evangeline, and offered it to her. Evangeline smiled as she quickly studied her own wedding photograph. In that moment, tears filled her eyes as she thought of the day Hutch came home with a wedding dress he'd asked Kizzy, Amoretta, and Calliope to make for Evangeline. Offering her the dress, a beautiful white fox fur muff, and matching hooded cape, Hutch had whisked Evangeline off to the new photographer man that had moved to Meadowlark Lake while Evangeline had been in Red Peak.

"It just won't do, Evie," Hutch had told her. "It just won't do, us not having our own wedding photograph. Especially considering your six-year-old sister has one."

A few tears of emotion provoked by the memory—of inconceivably deep love for Hutch and his profound consideration for her—trickled over Evangeline's cheek as she looked at the image of her handsome husband, dressed so eloquently in his suit and hat.

"Hold it up, Evie," Shay whispered.

And as Evangeline held up her wedding photograph to be displayed for all to see, Shay sang, "Then the last little girl had a dream . . . and she dreamed she was saying, 'I do.' And when she awoke, it was true!"

Spinning in the middle of the room then, looking like a shiny red top, Shay finished, "Happy three little girls dressed in blue!"

Everyone applauded with true admiration and emotion at Shay's performance. Having taken the tender song that Lawson Ipswich had sung to his three older daughters from the day they were each born, and then to Shay when she came to be his own, and linked it with Evangeline's, Amoretta's, and Calliope's wedding photos, Shay truly had performed a beautiful gift.

But as everyone kept applauding, Shay waved her hands in gesturing they should stop.

"Everyone settle down," the child giggled. "Now it's time for part two!"

"Oh, Shay, everyone's so tired, darling," Kizzy began.

"It will be worth it, Mama, don't worry," Shay assured her mother.

Then, going to the box again, Shay retrieved three folded pieces of fabric. Evangeline gasped in unison with Amoretta and Calliope as instant understanding simultaneously struck them all.

"Mrs. Montrose helped me make these, Daddy," Shay explained. "They're so you can start everything all over again." Unfolding one of the pieces of fabric, Shay held it up to herself and said, "See? This one is mine!" Unfolding the other two, she laid one each over Leonora and Peanna as they slept in her father's arms. "And these are for Leonora and Peanna."

As Kizzy fairly burst into weeping, Lawson's eyes filled with moisture as Shay hopped up into his lap and began to sing, "There were three little girls dressed in blue." Pausing she said, "Sing with me, Daddy!"

Tears streamed down Evangeline's cheeks as

her father's voice quivered as he joined Shay in singing, "Then one married and left only two."

By the next line of the song, everyone in the room was singing along, every woman in the room weeping.

"Then one fell in love with a boy . . . who loved her and gave her much joy. Then the last little girl had a dream . . . and she dreamed she was saying, 'I do.' And when she awoke it was true! Happy three little girls dressed in blue."

Hours later, as Evangeline lay in the arms of her handsome lover and husband in their bed in the little cottage in the Meadowlark Lake woods, Evangeline whispered, "I can't believe how wonderful you are to me, Hutch."

"What do you mean, sugar?" Hutch asked.

Evangeline shook her head where it lay against his warm, broad chest. "All of it, Hutch," she explained. "The telegrams and letters to Daddy for one. When you contacted him and told him we'd been married . . . and that you wanted me to love you but weren't sure I could be happy away from my family." She sat up in their bed and looked at him. "For Pete's sake, Hutch! You sold your livery in Red Peak and bought the one here from Lou Smith! You moved here, Hutch, after all you worked for . . . just so I could be close to my family."

Hutch shrugged. "So?" he asked. "I don't care where I am, Evangeline. As long as I'm with you."

Evangeline ran her fingers back through her long hair. "And this cottage," she said, shaking her head. "Buying the cottage from Daddy and Kizzy—and helping Calvin and Jennie and the baby, even Calvin's mother . . . all of them, moving here in the spring—and Calvin working for you at the livery."

Again Hutch shrugged. "The livery here is bigger than mine was in Red Peak. I need the help."

Evangeline brushed tears from her cheeks. "Even our wedding photograph . . . my gown! You overwhelm me with your heroics, Hutchner LaMontagne."

"You overwhelm me with the fact that you love me, Evie," Hutch said, sitting up and gathering her into his arms. "Why wouldn't I do everything in my power to make you happy? To make your life as happy and as filled with the company of everyone you love as it can be?"

"But I could never do so much for you, Hutch!" she exclaimed. "You make it impossible for me to repay you for all you do for me."

"Hey," Hutch said then, taking her face between his hands so that she would look directly at him. "You do everything for me, Evangeline. You love me, and that's more than I can ever repay you for. And besides, it's not about repaying things. It's about building the best life together that we can . . . for each other. We both make sacrifices, we both work hard at being lovers forever—not just husband and wife . . . truly best friends and lovers." He grinned, adding, "And didn't I tell you I'd make a good lover? That day I was teasing you at Jennie's?"

Evangeline giggled. "Yes, you did."

"And wasn't I right?" he teased.

"Yes, you were," she laughed. "And you're not too humble about it either."

"Now," he began, "come here, my raven-haired beauty."

Evangeline smiled as Hutch laid her back down on the bed, hovering over her as he studied her face.

"You know that I want at least three daughters, don't you?" he said, smiling.

"Why?" Evangeline asked—though she suspected she knew.

"So I can sing your father's song to them when I rock them to sleep at night," he admitted.

"Well, I'll see what I can do someday, all right?" Evangeline whispered as her hand moved to her tummy a moment. She didn't know for sure—at least not sure enough to tell Hutch and get his hopes up. But if her every month didn't appear again in two or three more weeks, she would visit Doctor Gregory to be certain, and then she would tell Hutch what her heart already knew was true.

Hutch chuckled. "And how about I do the best I can right now, hmm?"

"You're a scandalous man, Hutchner LaMontagne," Evangeline sighed as Hutch pressed a soft, caressive kiss to her neck.

"I'm a man in love with his wife, sugar," he sang against her ear. Then he quietly sang, "Then the last little girl had a dream . . . and she dreamed Hutch was saying, 'I do.' "

"And when she awoke it was true," Evangeline sang breathlessly. "Happy *me,* little girl dressed in blue."

AUTHOR'S NOTE

Okay, what's the phrase that people use when they ask a person to do something they know they really don't want to do, but figure they'll enjoy or accept in the end? Oh yeah! "Humor me, if you will."

I'll begin this author's note with that very phrase and beg you to *humor me, if you will.* I've included a couple of excerpts from two authors that I revere as my favorites, whose writing I believe can also be life-changing. I'm asking you to take just a minute or two and read (slowly and with the purpose of enjoyment) these excerpts before you read the rest of this author's note—please. Okay, here we go:

Description of Ichabod Crane, taken from *The Legend of Sleepy Hollow* by Washington Irving, now public domain, first published 1819–1820:

> He was tall, but exceedingly lank, with narrow shoulders, long arms and legs, hands that dangled a mile out of his sleeves, feet that might have served for shovels, and his whole frame most loosely hung together. His head was small, and flat at top, with huge ears, large green

glassy eyes, and a long snipe nose, so that it looked like a weathercock, perched upon his spindle neck, to tell which way the wind blew. To see him striding along the profile of a hill on a windy day, with his clothes bagging and fluttering about him, one might have mistaken him for the genius of famine descending upon the earth, or some scarecrow eloped from a cornfield.

An excerpt from my favorite poem, "The South-Wind and the Sun," by James Whitcomb Riley, now public domain, first published 1890:

O The South Wind and the Sun!
How each loved the other one—
Full of fancy—full folly—
Full of jollity and fun!
How they romped and ran about,
Like two boys when school is out,
With glowing face, and lisping lip,
Low laugh, and lifted shout!

And the South Wind—he was dressed
With a ribbon round his breast
That floated, flapped and fluttered
In a riotous unrest,
And a drapery of mist
From the shoulder and the wrist

Flowing backward with the motion
Of the waving hand he kissed.

And the Sun had on a crown
Wrought of gilded thistle-down,
And a scarf of velvet vapor,
And a raveled-rainbow gown;
And his tinsel-tangled hair,
Tossed and lost upon the air,
Was glossier and flossier
Than any anywhere.

These are examples of the kinds of things *I* like to read, my young bonnie lasses and my dashing handsome lads! Considered far too wordy (Irving) or far too fluffy (Riley) for most readers today, this type of writing I hail to be downright soul-soothing! I so miss this kind of beauty being in our world. I even miss the writing styles of authors such as Victoria Holt and Georgette Heyer!

I mean, how can anyone not love that description of Ichabod? Doesn't it just perfectly set his appearance in your mind? Even if you'd never seen Disney's animated version of *The Legend of Sleepy Hollow* or the movie starring Jeff Goldblum as Ichabod Crane, you'd know exactly what Ichabod looked like. Not only would you know what he looked like, but you'd also be left with the feeling of the time period, just as if you had been whisked back to 1820, you know?

And the poem! How can anyone keep from sighing with respite or smiling with joy after reading words woven together in such wonderment: "And the Sun had on a crown, wrought of gilded thistle-down, and a scarf of velvet vapor, and a raveled-rainbow gown." Okay, well admittedly maybe guys don't smile and feel respite at reading that. I'm thinking my husband would quirk an eyebrow and look at me like I'd lost my mind if I suggested he would be thrilled with this poem. Still, you know what I mean, right? These kinds of beauties are lost today!

But the world (as a whole) is what it is—has dumbed-down its vocabulary and ability to simply sink into a descriptive passage and bathe in truly savoring it, you know? That being said, however, I do not feel that you and I have given up on beauty and fluff in our reading. And in truth, that is what my goal is (and always has been) when writing my stories—to attempt to give my reader just a whiff of what I feel when I read Irving and Riley. I want a reader to feel happier when they're finished with one of my stories. I want words like *resplendent, caressively, ambrosia, autumn,* and *delight* to bounce around in someone's mind once they finished a book I've written. I just want *you* to feel happier and as if you've had a moment of escape from everything tugging at your mind.

To be honest, sometimes my goal for my readers does backfire on me. I can't remember where I saw this, but somewhere out there is a review of *A Crimson Frost* where the person simply wrote, "I'm not a fan of poetry."

Naturally, I was crushed! I don't know if the average person who doesn't write for a living knows how time-consuming and difficult the kind of poetry included in *A Crimson Frost* is to write! Believe me, I love to write poetry (as is evident in *Shackles of Honor* and the *Time of Aspen Falls* as well, right?), but it does take some time and concentration of thought. And to have the only comment in that review be, "I'm not a fan of poetry," was kind of crushing. I mean, what? Didn't she like the Crimson Knight when his shirt was off? And I was brave enough to make reference to his "navel." ☺

Of course, not everybody is a fan of poetry, and I totally get that. But long ago, most things a body had access to read were poems, sonnets, or derivatives, you know?

And yet there was to be a much greater purpose intended for those poems in *A Crimson Frost*, and my crushed ego was instantly healed when I received an e-mail from a reader and friend, informing me that her son (I believe he was in eighth grade at the time) had received a school assignment to memorize a poem and recite it in front of the class. Needless to say, he was less than thrilled about the whole project. Therefore, his mother (wise woman that she obviously was) suggested he memorize one of the poems from *A Crimson Frost*—you know, since a couple of them are epic where masculinity and battle are concerned. The boy actually liked the poem, memorized it, and pulled off a fabulous recitation. And that was worth more to me than any other review (good or bad) *A Crimson Frost* had ever received! Somewhere out there is a young man who at least *read* a poem in this day and age, right? And maybe it actually entertained him. I can't think of a better compliment than having an adolescent boy memorize one of my poems! (It's right up there with the college professor's wife who once told me that her literary professor husband really enjoyed my poetry! Fabulous!)

When I was in high school, I was given a similar assignment: to memorize a poem and recite it in front of the class. Well, remember as a kid when you'd get an assignment like that and realized you were already accidentally prepared? Loved that, didn't you? Anyway, thanks to my own mother, I had, years before, memorized a poem that she would often recite when doing this and that around the house. Some of you may be familiar with it. It was an epic tale—not quite politically correct by today's standards, but epic all the same. I will say that my recitation of it bordered on Anne Shirley quality and was well received by my classmates. It goes like this:

Ladies and gentlemen!
Hobos and tramps!
Cross-eyed mosquitoes
And bow-legged ants!

I come before you, to stand behind you,
to tell you a tale I've never heard before!

One dark day on a sunny night,
Two dead boys got up to fight!
Back to back they faced each other,
Drew their swords and shot each other!

A deaf policeman heard the noise
And came and killed the two dead boys.

If you don't believe this lie—it's true!
Ask the blind man . . .
He saw it, too!

Yes, an epically ridiculous moment in my high school career! How embarrassing! But at least I pulled an A+ out of it! ☺

By now you're wondering why I'm going on and on about poetry, my high school career, and reiterating my purpose in writing stories for you. Well, as you know the past few years have been so wrought with stress for Kevin and me—wrought with health problems, business drama, one of my sons being away from home for two whole years (I know you've heard all this whining before, blah blah, poor me). Even though I'd pop up for air here and there and think, *Oh, I'm feeling better now! I'm even thinking better now!*—it wasn't true!

To be honest, I think a ton of the reasons I struggled was pressures where my writing was concerned. Some readers want less detail, some want books to be shorter, some want books to be longer, some don't like a few cuss words, some want more sizzle, some want less sizzle, and some don't even like poetry! And let me tell you, it gets in your head, you know?

However, as I was finishing up *The Romancing of Evangeline Ipswich*, a lot of things began to fall into place. My editor/friend, for one thing, has helped me, guided me into writing what I want to write for my readers, but in a manner that better fits with what readers demand these days. I've also found a balance in my life where reading for my own entertainment is a possibility for me again. I had missed that! I hadn't read a book (other than comics or children's books) for literally years! And I'm finding that I do enjoy reading again. Another thing is that my son who has been away for two years is coming home, and that means that the hole that was punched in my heart when he left will be healed and not so distracting to me. Kevin has found a new balance in our business side of things too. 2014 was a precarious year. We almost bought the farm! Oh, wait, that's a death reference. I think I mean we almost lost our shirts! (Which, in Kevin's handsome muscular state of body wouldn't be so bad—but in mine, yikes!)

Another thing I learned was that I'm what's known as empathic or an empath—not in the supernatural sense, of course, just the personality characteristic sense that many of us have. I think you probably know what empathic or empath means, but just in case, here are a couple of little definitions:

> **Empathic:** The psychological recognition of the feelings, thoughts, or attitudes of others.

> **Empath:** One who is capable of actually feeling the emotions of others in spite of the fact that they themselves are not experiencing the same condition.

So imagine that you're empathic and you have a friend who calls you and tells you her mother is passing away. That's right—the tears flow, the heart aches, just like your friend's! That's what happens to me! I mean, I always knew that

that sort of thing happened to me, but I never understood how it can drain a person of energy— distract a mind and heart from doing tasks that need doing.

Take for instance the time about fifteen years ago. Having had multiple phone calls one day, I began to feel pretty stressed out. I attributed my stress to three phone calls in particular: (1) A casual friend called to ask me to write a character reference for her to be used in her defense at a trial for embezzlement. Keep in mind I knew the lady had some challenges (i.e., a son with some physical ailments that had found him addicted to prescription drugs and in and out of rehab), but I had no idea she had embezzled money from her place of employment to help pay for his rehab! (2) A casual friend called me to tell me that her son was being charged with raping his girlfriend. (3) A good friend called to tell me that her eldest daughter had come to her and her husband and informed them of some decisions she'd made that were devastating to the family. And that was just three of the phone calls that day. Well, I went about my day, taking care of the kids, fixing supper, even going to a friend's house and visiting a while. But later than night—long after I'd gone to bed—I suddenly woke up with the feeling that I was going to throw up! And not just throw up—have, you know, Montezuma's revenge, as well—simultaneously! I raced to the bathroom, sat down on the potty, and as the pain in my body and nausea grew and grew, I began to pray that I wouldn't die! I couldn't breathe, I was perspiring like crazy, and all of a sudden, I woke up facedown on my bathroom rug, thinking, *I'm sure glad I washed these rugs today!*

It took several more incidents of that gravity and a few years for me to figure out that I wasn't battling some crazy five-minute flu. I was being overpowered by anxiety caused by the way I absorbed everyone else's stress and feelings.

For a long time I thought I was alone in having these kinds of physical reactions to having empathy for others. I have since learned that I'm not the only one dealing with it. I've found some ways to keep from passing out in the bathroom in the middle of the night (although I do keep my bathroom rugs regularly laundered, just in case). (P.S. Guess what? Research has also found that people who struggle with social phobia are usually highly empathic. Voila! Or as my father-in-law would say, Viola!)

Again, what does this have to do with Evangeline's story? Well, *The Romancing of Evangeline Ipswich* is the last book I'm ever going to write that I don't thoroughly enjoy writing! It's also the first book I've finished in a long time while, after years of chaos, either things have started to settle down and fall into place a bit more, or I'm just in a healthy state of mind—or both. It's also the first book I finished in years while giving myself and my brain any reprieve from thinking about the story at all (i.e., watching favorite shows, movies, or reading). It's the first book in over two years that I've written with the knowledge that my youngest son is almost home and therefore my family will feel complete again. And it's the first book I've written in a long, long time where, if the need had arisen (which it didn't) for me to use the word navel, I wouldn't have been scared to use it for fear of angry reviews or e-mails!

I'll wrap it up now, so that, if you're still awake and reading, you can journey on to whatever tasks are vying for your attention. But before I give you the snippets of Evangeline's story that you might actually *want* to read, I will include one last quote from Washington Irving, because when I read this wonderful explanation of why he had written what he did at the end of one of his stories, I read it in awed wonderment—for his purpose in writing had been exactly what my own purpose is—simply to amuse, to chase away sorrow!

P.S. I also love that one of Washington Irving's pennames was "Geoffrey Crayon"!

Taken from *The Sketch Book of Geoffrey Crayon, Gent., The Christmas Dinner*, by Washington

Irving, now public domain, first published 1819–1820:

But enough of Christmas and its gambols; it is time for me to pause in this garrulity. Methinks I hear the questions asked by my graver readers, "To what purpose is all this? How is the world to be made wiser by this talk?" Alas! Is there not wisdom enough extant for the instruction of the world? And if not, are there not thousands of abler pens laboring for its improvement? It is so much pleasanter to please than to instruct, to play the companion rather than the preceptor.

What, after all, is the mite of wisdom that I could throw into the mass of knowledge! Or how am I sure that my sagest deductions may be safe guides for the opinions of others? But in writing to amuse, if I fail the only evil is in my own disappointment. If, however, I can by any lucky chance, in these days of evil, rub out one wrinkle from the brow of care or beguile the heavy heart of one moment of sorrow; if I can now and then penetrate through the gathering film of misanthropy, prompt a benevolent view of human nature, and make my reader more in good-humor with his fellow-beings and himself, surely, surely, I shall not then have written entirely in vain.

Yours,
Marcia Lynn McClure

Snippet #1—Hutch's name: I can't believe I almost forgot to include this in my snippets! You see, I had just finished the first chapter of *The Romancing of Evangeline Ipswich* and had sent it to my daughter to see if she liked it. Well, lo and behold, she called me and revealed that the first name of my hero for the story (which at the time was "Blank" LaMontagne instead of Hutchner "Hutch" LaMontagne) was the name she was going to give to her next little baby boy (if she has one). Being that she and I are so similar in our thought processes, I had inadvertently fallen in love with a name that she had too! However, being that I would *love* to have a grandson named "Blank," I opted to change the hero's name from Blank to Hutch! I love the name Hutch too— so it's a win-win for me! And hopefully I'll get another little grandson one day named Blank!

Snippet #2—Why yes, Doctor Swayze's name is Patrick—Patrick Swayze! And yes, I was thinking of Patrick Swayze the day I named him. (Marcia Dork Alert #378!)

Snippet #3—While writing *The Romancing of Evangeline Ipswich*, I'd occasionally collapse on the sofa for a bit of downtime in watching a little series called *Animal House*. It's a reality show—kind of old, actually, filmed in 2004—about a rescue shelter for animals located in New York. Well, while enjoying an episode of *Animal House* one evening—an episode focused on a sweet little three-legged dog rescued after Hurricane Sandy—I thought, *Hey, Hutch should have a three-legged dog!* Truly, I think it was my way of adopting the three-legged dog on *Animal House* by proxy. And so Hutch has Jones—an adorable, brown, three-legged dog. (FYI—The show did say that the three-legged dog featured on *Animal House* found a good home. So you can relax about that and not worry.)

Snippet #4—As you've probably already guessed, Evangeline's delicious chicken stew and herb biscuits are based on a family favorite of ours. I can't even remember where I originally came across this recipe, but over the years I tweaked it until it is what it is today. My kids love this recipe! It's the ultimate "comfort food" stew, and the soft, herby biscuits (which are actually cooked right on top of the stew) are the crowning *yum-yum* of the recipe. Knowing how we all love comfort food, I thought I'd include the recipe here, just in case you want to try it. Enjoy!

CHICKEN STEW AND HERB BISCUITS

Ingredients for Stew:
1 to 2 pounds chicken
2 to 4 cups carrots (sliced)
2 to 3 medium potatoes (cubed)
1 onion (finely chopped)
3 to 4 celery stalks (chopped)
1 teaspoon rubbed sage
½ teaspoon dried basil
5 to 6 cups chicken broth
Salt and pepper to taste

Boil chicken until it is thoroughly cooked. Remove chicken from broth and set aside. Add enough water to broth to make 5 to 6 cups of liquid. Add vegetables, herbs, salt, and pepper (to taste) to broth and boil until vegetables are tender. Cut chicken into bite-size pieces and add into stew. Set stew to simmering.

Ingredients for Herb Biscuits:
2 cups flour
3 teaspoons baking powder
1 teaspoon salt
1½ teaspoons thyme
1 teaspoon dried parsley
¼ cup butter
1 cup milk

Mix dry ingredients, and cut in butter with fork. Add milk, and mix into soft, sticky dough. Drop by large spoonfuls (10 to 12) onto simmering stew. (Watch your heat setting; this will stick badly if the bottom of the pan is too hot.) Simmer 10 minutes uncovered, and then cover and simmer for 10 more minutes. Remove biscuits from stew and place on separate serving plate. Serve stew and biscuits together.

Snippet #5—A secret tragedy was narrowly avoided! When Evangeline's and Hutch's story was first in my mind, I'm going to confess to you that Jennie died during childbirth. I know, right?!?! How could I have imagined such a thing? Well, tragically, those things did, and do, happen. But Jennie's death just didn't set well with me. I wanted Evangeline's story to be as happy ever after as Amoretta's and Calliope's, and I knew if Jennie died, that couldn't happen for that would leave Evangeline with another tragic loss in her own life and also rob Hutch of his one sibling. Thankfully I woke up one morning having been able to pull myself out of my strange, tragic way of thinking, and whew! Close call, right?

Snippet #6—In the fall and winter of 2006, two major occurrences unfolded while we were living in Monument, Colorado. The first was what is now known as "The Blizzards of 2006!" Beginning in mid-October that year, we had begun to have tons of snowfall! This made some everyday things very difficult for us—things like getting our boys to school when our quarter of a mile driveway had three or four feet of snow covering it every morning because of snow and wind. But beginning on December 20 of that year, the blizzards really hit! I-25 was closed, as were multiple other major thoroughfares. Maybe you're thinking, *That's not so bad! Just grab some hot chocolate, a blanket, and a movie!* But you see, our daughter, Sandy, was getting married on the December 28—and she, her fiancé, and other family members were driving in or flying at that time. You'll be so relieved to know that I'm going to make a long story short and tell you what happened in telegram form. More blizzards hit December 28 and 29. Sandy and Soren married on December 28. Guests and family from out of town barely made it through the whiteout conditions to reach our home just after ceremony. Only one fender bender between the cars—mine sliding into Kevin's. Twenty-one people snowed in at our house for three days— wedding reception canceled. Reception food fed the masses, thank goodness. Sixty-six rolls of toilet paper distributed and used during the three-day snow-in. Kevin spent nine hours on a tractor clearing our driveway, and we literally pushed the first van of guests through the drifts on either side to get them out. Another family made it out, only to find I-25 closed at the New Mexico–Colorado border. Laundry of bedding took me a week to finish up. And the most important thing of all—my poor, beautiful daughter never got *any* wedding photos at her wedding or reception! Sandy does have some lovely wedding photos that a friend of hers took once Sandy and Soren were back at college. But it never healed the disappointment of not having actual wedding photos, you know? And there you have it—the reason why Hutch made darn sure Evangeline had a beautiful wedding photo of him and her—even though it was taken after they'd been married!

Snippet #7—My mom's "Earthly Story." For my last snippet, I'm going to include a little excerpt from a small but wonderful personal history my mom jotted down over twenty years ago when she was laid up after foot surgery. In 1991, grabbing a yellow legal notepad and a pen, Mom hurriedly recorded (in shorthand, mind you) some of her memories of growing up, marriage, having children, and other life experiences. Being that my mom now suffers from dementia and Alzheimer's, this record (which she *did* transcribe into something I can read, thank heaven!)—a short, incomplete, but cherished and profound story of her life—is one of my greatest and most beloved treasures! And being that all three books in the Three Little Girls Dressed in Blue trilogy were dedicated to my mom and written with her ever in mind, I thought it would be wonderful to share a bit of insight into my mom's life (i.e., much of the heart of my initial inspiration in writing this trilogy). The reference in this excerpt addressed to "Skeeter" was to me—being that Skeeter was my nickname and the name by which everyone called me until I was more than nineteen years old.

After we moved to South Street, Sharon and I slept in the attic. I'm sure it was very hot in the summer, but I remember the winter. In the winter, our bed would be so cold that we would curl up in tight little balls trying to stay warm. Later in the night, if we wanted to stretch out, no matter how badly we were cramped up, we couldn't put our feet into the freezing cold reaches of our bed. To compound the situation, our covers were of the make-'em-out-of-whatever-you-had quilts. And, it appears that "heavy" used to mean "warmth." The ones on our bed were made from large wool and denim scraps with no fluffy batting like we have today. They were all weight and no warmth. Since then I have read that heavy blankets cause one to wake up tired. Every time you breathe, you have to lift all that weight. I believe it. Whenever snow fell, it would sift through the cracks in the shingles on the roof and fall onto our faces.

At one time, my Uncle Rusty (Hubert Switzler) was staying with us. We had a snowstorm during the night. The next morning my dad asked Uncle Rusty how he had slept. Uncle Rusty retorted, "(Blankety Blank), it snowed in my face all night!" As was his usual characteristic, my dad bent over with laughter.

The attic was a neat place to sneak away to for a little privacy (especially since I didn't have a window seat). One Christmas season when I was still very young, I came home from school, slipped up to the attic, and made red and green construction paper chains. (Yes, Skeeter, we had construction paper when I was young.) I was having so much fun I hardly noticed I had turned into a block of ice until Mom found me.

Then winters arrived with cold and wind again and snow and ice and the car not starting and Dad having to walk two and a half miles to work and having to do chores night and morning half frozen; breaking ice on the horse tank so the animals could drink, feeding horses and cows and pigs and chickens and milking cows. Days when Mom would keep us home from school because it was so cold and maybe just because she wanted some company.

I was never required to help outside except for getting in the kindling, coal, and water. My dad was a staunch believer that women's work was in the house and maybe in the garden but not out in the cold tending livestock except in an emergency, and not working away from home. He seemed to have a feeling that his mother literally had been worked to death after they moved from Kansas to Colorado. She died at age 62 of a stroke.

Christmases were great fun at our house. Santa Claus bought us each a nice gift and filled our stockings with oranges, candy, and nuts. Mom and Dad always gave us each a couple of small gifts, usually clothes and some little trinket.

The Christmas of 1954, my senior year, I got a Lane cedar chest, which I still have. Sharon got a piano, which she still has, Wayne got a .22 rifle, and Russell got a pair of boots, a black cowboy outfit, and a toy gun belt with two holsters and toy guns. After Dad started managing the Lemon's Feed Store, he got a bonus twice a year one of which was around Christmas. This year I'm sure most if not all of his bonus went for Christmas. I don't know how much they paid for my cedar chest, but I do know Sharon's piano was $90.

Other gifts I remember receiving from my parents are two *Shirley Temple* books and *Patty O'Neal on the Airways*, which I still have. Another book they gave me at some time was *The Swiss Family Robinson*. These may have been birthday gifts. These are the only books I ever remember owning until recent years except for my scriptures and some church books and *The Little Red Hen*, which Aunt Opal gave me while we were still at Westcliffe.

Other Christmas gifts I remember receiving are a Bible, which I requested, a jewelry box, a string of "pearls," and a pink sweater set. The last three were all received at one Christmas I think in 1953. Normally, we never received a lot of gifts like so many do today, but it was a lot to us. I also have the remains of a big baby doll that still cries but whose two front teeth have fallen inside. She also has a broken leg. My sister stepped on it. Guess I should have kept her off the attic floor. ☺

As another rambling, pointless sidenote—the baby doll my mom mentions is in my possession now. Some twenty-five years ago, I couldn't stand the thought of the poor baby doll being buried in a trunk out in the garage! I mean, how on earth was she able to breathe in there? Nightmare, right? Knowing that her smothering baby doll in the trunk horrified me so, Mom dug the precious doll out of the trunk so she could breathe more easily and gave her to me. That old, banged-up composite doll with the shattered and then glued-back-together leg had now been a part of my own family for over twenty-five years. Today she sits in our front room, in an old wicker dolly sled, wearing a pretty Christmas plaid dress, a white baby bonnet, and a white faux fur cape, with her small, well-loved hands tucked into a white faux fur muff. Although the poor little thing kind of always creeps out little kids (even my own kids when they were really little), my little eighteen-month-old grandson seems to love the baby doll and probably thinks she's real—because for about six months now, whenever he's over, he always talks to her, rocks her little sleigh, and gives her a kiss on the mouth! Is that adorable or what? When my mom was still able to remember that I had the doll, she always told me that she was so glad her baby doll was out where she could breathe well and be loved. I love my mom so much!

Snippet #8—And now for my final snippet, which is me endeavoring to leave you with some added loveliness! Finishing *The Romancing of Evangeline Ipswich* found me feeling liberated of sorts. I'd spent almost two years in that same venue of writing (western, same basic characters being the Ipswich family), and I was more than ready to move on to a new project. And so, I leave you with the poem that I included an excerpt from in the beginning of this author's note—because it uplifts me and is such a beautiful piece of beauty and respite to me, and it helped me in finding my enjoyment in writing Evangeline's story. That's how thoroughly I love the words James Whitcomb Riley put together so eloquently in that poem. Thus, being that the poem is public domain, and therefore I'm able to print it here for you, I have! I hope you'll take the time to savor it—and not just once but any-time you feel your mind, heart, and soul need a lift.

*I've listed a few words, and their definitions, that may be unfamiliar to you because they aren't commonly used anymore to allow you to read the poem more smoothly.

Kine—"Cows collectively."
Bobolink and Killdee are both birds.
Freak—in this instance means "to fleck or streak randomly."
Muscadine—"wine grapes."
Shallop—"a sailboat."

THE SOUTH WIND AND THE SUN!

O The South Wind and the Sun!
How each loved the other one
Full of fancy—full folly—
Full of jollity and fun!
How they romped and ran about,
Like two boys when school is out,
With glowing face, and lisping lip,
Low laugh, and lifted shout!

And the South Wind—he was dressed
With a ribbon round his breast
That floated, flapped and fluttered
In a riotous unrest,
And a drapery of mist
From the shoulder and the wrist
Flowing backward with the motion
Of the waving hand he kissed.

And the Sun had on a crown
Wrought of gilded thistle-down,
And a scarf of velvet vapor,
And a raveled-rainbow gown;
And his tinsel-tangled hair,
Tossed and lost upon the air,
Was glossier and flossier
Than any anywhere.

And the South Wind's eyes were two
Little dancing drops of dew,
As he puffed his cheeks, and pursed his lips,
And blew and blew and blew!
And the Sun's—like diamond-stone,
Brighter yet than ever known,
As he knit his brows and held his breath,
And shone and shone and shone!

And this pair of merry fays
Wandered through the summer days;
Arm-in-arm they went together
Over heights of morning haze—
Over slanting slopes of lawn
They went on and on and on,
Where the daisies looked like star-tracks
Trailing up and down the dawn.

And where'er they found the top
Of a wheat-stalk droop and lop
They chucked it underneath the chin

And praised the lavish crop,
Till it lifted with the pride
Of the heads it grew beside,
And then the South Wind and the Sun
Went onward satisfied.

Over meadow-lands they tripped,
Where the dandelions dipped
In crimson foam of clover-bloom,
And dripped and dripped and dripped;
And they clinched the bumble-stings,
Gauming honey on their wings,
And bundling them in lily-bells,
With maudlin murmurings.

And the humming-bird that hung
Like a jewel up among
The tilted honeysuckle-horns,
They mesmerized, and swung
In the palpitating air,
Drowsed with odors strange and rare,
And with whispered laughter, slipped away,
And left him hanging there.

And they braided blades of grass
Where the truant had to pass;
And they wriggled through the rushes
And the reeds of the morass,
Where they danced, in rapture sweet,
O'er the leaves that laid a street

Of undulant mosaic for
The touches of their feet.

By the brook with mossy brink
Where the cattle came to drink.
They trilled and piped and whistled
With the thrush and bobolink,
Till the kine in listless pause,
Switched their tails in mute applause,
With lifted heads and dreamy eyes,
And bubble-dripping jaws.

And where the melons grew,
Streaked with yellow, green and blue
These jolly sprites went wandering
Through spangled paths of dew;
And the melons, here and there,
They made love to, everywhere
Turning their pink souls to crimson
With caresses fond and fair.

Over orchard walls they went,
Where the fruited boughs were bent
Till they brushed the sward beneath them
Where the shine and shadow blent;
And the great green pear they shook
Till the sallow hue forsook
Its features, and the gleam of gold
Laughed out in every look.

And they stroked the downy cheek
Of the peach, and smoothed it sleek,
And flushed it into splendor;
And with many an elfish freak,
Gave the russet's rust a wipe—
Prankt the rambo with a stripe,
And the wine-sap blushed its reddest
As they spanked the pippins ripe.

Through the woven ambuscade
That the twining vines had made,
They found the grapes, in clusters,
Drinking up the shine and shade—
Plumpt like tiny skins of wine,
With a vintage so divine
That the tongue of fancy tingled
With the tang of muscadine.

And the golden-banded bees,
Droning o'er the flowery leas,
They bridled, reigned, and rode away
Across the fragrant breeze,
Till in hollow oak and elm
They had groomed and stabled them
In waxen stalls oozed with dews
Of rose and lily-stem.

Where the dusty highway leads,
High above the wayside weeds
They sowed the air with butterflies

Like blooming flower-seeds,
Till the dull grasshopper sprung
Half a man's height up, and hung
Tranced in the heat, with whirring wings,
And sung and sung and sung!

And they loitered, hand in hand,
Where the snipe along the sand
Of the river ran to meet them
As the ripple meets the land,
Till the dragon-fly, in light
Gauzy armor, burnished bright,
Came tilting down the waters
In a wild, bewildered flight.

And they heard the killdee's call,
And afar, the waterfall,
But the rustle of a falling leaf
They heard above it all;
And the trailing willow crept
Deeper in the tide that swept
The leafy shallop to the shore,
And wept and wept and wept!

And the fairy vessel veered
From its moorings—tacked and steered
For the centre of the current
Sailed away and disappeared:
And the burthen that it bore
From the long-enchanted shore—

"Alas! The South Wind and the Sun!"
I murmur evermore.

For the South Wind and the Sun,
Each so loves the other one,
For all his jolly folly
And frivolity and fun,
That our love for them they weigh
As their fickle fancies may,
And when at last we love them most,
They laugh and sail away.

~James Whitcomb Riley

ABOUT THE AUTHOR

Marcia Lynn McClure's intoxicating succession of novels, novellas, and e-books—including *Dusty Britches*, *The Whispered Kiss*, *The Haunting of Autumn Lake*, and *The Bewitching of Amoretta Ipswich*—has established her as one of the most favored and engaging authors of true romance. Her unprecedented forte in weaving captivating stories of western, medieval, regency, and contemporary amour void of brusque intimacy has earned her the title "The Queen of Kissing."

Marcia, who was born in Albuquerque, New Mexico, has spent her life intrigued with people, history, love, and romance. A wife, mother, grandmother, family historian, poet, and author, Marcia Lynn McClure spins her tales of splendor for the sake of offering respite through the beauty, mirth, and delight of a worthwhile and wonderful story.

Center Point Large Print
600 Brooks Road / PO Box 1
Thorndike, ME 04986-0001 USA

(207) 568-3717

US & Canada:
1 800 929-9108
www.centerpointlargeprint.com